PATH OF THE
THUNDERBIRD

PATH OF THE THUNDERBIRD

A GRAND CANYON ADVENTURE

Sara Miller and Pat Toole

ILLUSTRATIONS BY
Scott Brundage

Grand Canyon Association

Grand Canyon Association

P.O. Box 399,
Grand Canyon, AZ 86023
(800) 858-2808
www.grandcanyon.org

Composed and Printed in the United States of America

Production Management and Editing by Theresa Howell
Designed by David Jenney Design

ISBN 978-1-934656-86-0

To every child
who has hiked farther,
climbed higher, or dreamed bigger
than they ever thought possible.

—S.M. & P.T.

IF YOU HAD TO PICK TWO THINGS
to keep you alive at the bottom of the biggest hole in the
world, what would you pick? The train chugged up the hill,
and we inched closer to Grand Canyon National Park. We
had no idea how important our choices would be.

"Really, Nate? Only two?" Oz asked.

My best friend's real name is Oscar, but he hates it, so
he started calling himself Oz after we read the *Wizard of Oz*.

"You can keep two important things, but we need to
vote on everything else." Our backpacks bulged on the metal shelf above our train seats. "Kira and I researched this.
Each of us should carry no more than twenty pounds. That's
eighty pounds between the four of us. Yours must weigh a
million, Oz."

One by one we grabbed our packs and put them at our
feet. We unloaded the supplies for our adventure. Flashlights, sunscreen, and water bottles covered the table in
front of us.

"My mom made me bring this trash bag as extra rain
gear." Oz handed it to me. "We can put the rejects in here."

"I don't need these ten sets of underwear *my* mom forced me to take. I could wear the same pair for a week." I tossed half my underwear into the trash bag.

We piled our must-haves in front of us.

Me: notebook, waterproof maps

Oz: cell phone, black plastic box

Hope: purple folder, mini photo album

Kira: binoculars, red yarn tied around a bullet

"Is that a necklace? Do you always wear a bullet around your neck?" Oz held up his hands and leaned back. "No one mess with Kira when we're on the trail."

She squeezed the yarn in her hand. "It's fake. Besides it's from Gramps…so I'll never forget the condors."

I wasn't sure how a fake bullet could make her think about condors. To be honest, I don't think much about birds at all, especially ones who look like angry turkeys.

Kira had tears in her eyes. I punched Oz so he'd be quiet. "Bullets and birds? How do those two things go together?" Oz asked. Sometimes he can't take a hint.

My cousin Kira and her friend Hope sat next to each other in seats that faced ours. Hope put her arm around Kira. "You know about Kira's science project, don't you? Responsible hunting with copper bullets?"

How would Oz know? I barely remembered the details of Kira's project. I only see my cousin three times a year, and science fair projects aren't usually what we talk about. I did remember she was the only sixth grader from her school to move on to the state science fair.

"If the hunters are shooting the condors, why does it matter what the bullets are made from? Aren't they going to die anyway?" Oz asked. I had to admit it was a good question.

Kira took a deep breath. "The hunters aren't shooting the condors. They're hunting for food…like deer. But all bullets used to be made from lead."

"So?" Oz said.

"Condors are scavengers, and they eat the dead animals with bits of shot still in them. The condors can't digest the shot, and the lead in it can poison them. Gramps helped promote responsible hunting with these copper bullets," Kira explained.

My cousin is the science genius of the family.

"Gross. That bullet was in some animal?" Oz pretended to throw up. "I didn't think girls liked gross stuff."

"Oz, give it a rest. Besides, it's fake. Let's get through the rest of this stuff. Those binoculars look heavy, Kira."

"These are non-negotiable. A good scientist needs her tools. How can I see any condors without these?"

"Let's vote," I said. "All in favor of Kira keeping her stuff?"

Three 'ayes' sounded together. Gran's head popped over the seat behind me.

"What are the four of you doing back here?" She glanced at the pile in front of us.

"We're voting to see which items stay in our packs and which ones are dead weight." Kira put the yarn necklace over her head.

"That's smart," Gran said. "On the train platform, you were crumpling under the weight of those packs."

The train platform was in Williams, Arizona, where we boarded the Grand Canyon Railway for the two-and-a-half hour trip to Grand Canyon. Gramps knew all about Grand

Canyon because he was an ornithologist, a bird scientist, who studied the California condors who lived there. That's why Kira is obsessed with those birds. Kira and I had been planning this trip with our grandparents for a year. But then, Gramps got sick.

He was the first person I ever knew who died. I'm still sad sometimes, but I know that Gran feels that way all the time. I think it's like if your hand got chopped off. You would still think it was there to pick up your fork, but you would reach out and find nothing at the end of your arm anymore. That's how I think she feels without Gramps, but she insisted we go on the trip after he died.

Gran patted my shoulder. "Glad to see you're taking charge of things, Nate. I'll leave you to it."

Kira nudged her friend. "You're next, Hope."

Hope tapped her folder. "I keep paper in here so I can write letters to my grandmother."

"Why don't you just send her an e-mail?" I asked.

Kira shook her head. "Duh, do you see any computers around here?"

"It wouldn't make any difference. My grandmother won't even touch computers. She's not like Gran."

"Hope writes *real* letters to her twice a week. With stamps and everything."

"I'm glad Gran lives close to me. I stink at writing letters," I said. "Do you write to her in English?"

"Mostly, sometimes I throw a little Havasupai in there because it makes my grandmother happy," Hope said.

"Hava-what?" Oz raised his eyebrows.

Hope grinned. "It's not that hard. Ha-va-su-pai. It means

'people of the blue-green water.' It's the name of my native language and also my tribe."

"That's awesome! I wish I was part of a tribe," Oz said.

I laughed. "Your tribe would be the people of glowing television screens."

"Nah. The people of outdoor survival." Oz pushed his arms up and down like a weight lifter.

"Outdoor survival? You mean that TV show? How does watching some crazy guy survive in the jungle make you an outdoor survival expert?" Somehow I couldn't imagine my friend surviving on his own in the wild.

"Just wait until we get into the canyon and you see all the things I've learned from Wildman," Oz said.

I didn't want to get him started on a Wildman rant, so I asked Hope, "What's the deal with this photo album?"

"It goes everywhere I go." Hope crossed her arms.

"Are you the trip photographer? Did you bring a camera, too?" Oz grinned and widened his eyes like he was posing.

"It's filled with pictures of my family," Hope clutched the book to her chest.

"We don't need to vote on the album or Hope's folder because we don't mess with family stuff." Kira looked at the trash bag I held. "We do need to make Nate get rid of something, though."

"I already put in all the extra clothes my mom packed for me," I said. "All I have left are these maps and my notebook with our trip schedule. We'll need those."

"Are you sure you don't have something else hidden in your bag?" Oz stuck his hand inside my pack. "What's this?"

"Oh, that's nothing."

5

Oz undid the snaps on the black leather case and showed everyone my drafting tools.

"What are these things? They look like ancient torture devices," Oz said.

Kira smiled. "Only if you hate math. What are you going to do with this stuff while we're hiking?"

"I thought I might use them to draw maps."

"Don't you have enough already?" She pointed at my stack of topographic maps. "I don't think you need to be drawing any more. All in favor of Nate dumping his tools?"

"How am I ever going to be a cartographer if you won't let me make—" Before I even finished I heard three 'ayes.' I tossed the case into the trash bag.

"Now for Oz," I said, before they found something else of mine to veto. "We're heading into Grand Canyon, not the Apple Store at the mall."

Oz's face turned red, the same color as his hair.

"I can't live without my gadgets. Besides, my mom says that I should call her if we have an emergency."

"Umm, Oz? I don't think your cell phone is going to work in the canyon," Kira said.

"We don't know that." Oz picked up the black box next to his phone. "And…" He unfolded a plastic handle from the side of the box and cranked it. "I've got a hand-powered cell phone charger in case I can't plug in."

"Dude, we're camping. Are you going to plug it into a tree?" I asked.

Oz shoved his stuff back into his bag. "What about Gran? Don't we get to vote on her stuff?"

She isn't Oz's grandma, but he calls her Gran and spends

as much time at her house as I do.

"Pack everything up, guys. It looks like we're here," said Gran.

The conductor's voice came on the loudspeaker and announced that the train was approaching the historic Grand Canyon Train Depot. We had finally arrived.

Kira and Hope marched toward the door. Oz and I waited at the bottom of the stairs to help Gran. Her gray braid bounced as she jumped down the stairs two at a time and ignored our outstretched hands.

Gran's not like other grandparents. She's crazy enough to take four twelve-year-olds on a trip to Grand Canyon. She runs marathons and her hobby is rock climbing, so she created a training program for us to help us get ready for our trip. We climbed bleachers and walked five miles every day. All summer and most of the school year, Gran and I showed up at Oz's house with our trekking poles. He hated those walks, but by the end of school year, we could go five miles in less than one hour.

Five miles sounds pretty easy, but our hike would be epic: twenty-four miles. 14.3 miles down from the North Rim and 9.6 miles back up to the South Rim. But it's not all flat like the sidewalks in my neighborhood. We would also climb down 6,000 feet and back up 4,500 feet. I mapped it out when Kira and I spent winter break planning our routes.

"Where is it? Seems like it would be hard to miss the biggest hole in the world," Oz said.

We were in front of an old log building. I was also surprised we couldn't see the canyon yet. Lots of passengers waited for luggage. We put on our backpacks and headed up a hill with stone steps. At the top of the stairs was a building like the pueblos we studied in our American Indian unit at school.

"We must be close. Look at all those people ahead," Kira said.

When we saw the crowds, we all ran. We squeezed between the people and stopped at a stone wall that was shorter than my waist. There it was—Grand Canyon.

It was like something took a huge bite out of the Earth with miles and miles of rocks: gray, red, and green. The one thing the maps don't show you is how tiny you'll feel when you see it. It's so much bigger in real life. I knew that the Colorado River was down there somewhere, like a snake winding through the canyon. We couldn't see it yet, though.

"Check out that ranger over there. What's she doing?" Oz yelled.

The ranger held a metal pole with rods sticking out of the sides in an H-shape. She wore a pair of blue headphones attached to a bag slung over her shoulder. With the antenna in front of her, she spun in a slow circle.

"What's that?" Hope asked.

"It's radio telemetry. I learned about it in my science fair project," Kira said. "She's tracking signals from a radio transmitter on an animal."

Kira had a death grip on the binoculars she held to her eyes. "She must be tracking a condor. People see them on the South Rim all the time."

"Is that all you think about?" Oz asked.

"This might be my only chance to see one in the wild." We peered into the canyon below. I was surprised there weren't any birds. Maybe they were too small to see in this giant crack in the ground.

The ranger folded up the antenna, and Kira gasped. "Oh no. She lost the radio signal. Condors can soar for miles, so it must have moved beyond the telemetry range or maybe deeper into the canyon."

The canyon was definitely deep, and we didn't have wings. How were we going to make it all the way down there, and more importantly, how were we going to make it back up again?

Gran interrupted my thoughts. "Oh, I almost forgot." She set her pack on the ground and unzipped the front pocket. "I know it's in here somewhere."

"What is it, Gran?" Kira asked.

"On the day Gramps died, he gave me a package. Inside was a letter addressed to the four of you with today's date on it."

Gran handed me the blue envelope. It was wrinkled, but I smoothed it out and read: To Nate, Kira, Oz, and Hope. To be opened on May 20.

"Have you read it?" I asked Gran.

She shook her head "No, but Gramps did say something about a mystery he hoped you would be able to solve."

I STARED AT THE LETTER. Hand-drawn sketches of birds, rocks, and squiggly lines covered the margins. Gramps' scratchy handwriting filled the middle of the page.

"Are you going to read it to us?" Kira asked.

I tightened my grip on the paper, took a deep breath, and read:

Dear Kids,

Welcome to Grand Canyon. By now you've peered down from the South Rim and had your first glimpse of the glories that await you. But the rim is only the tip of the iceberg. There are mysteries waiting to be discovered within the canyon that are far greater than anything you could imagine.

We've been planning this trip for more than a year. I wish I were there with you, but there is a way we can still experience Grand Canyon together. Do you remember how I loved to create treasure hunts? Think of this as my last one—specifically designed for the four of you. At the end, is a treasure far greater than any I've given you before.

All of you have an important role in this adventure. Nate, you see yourself as a navigator; Kira—a scientist; Oz—a survivalist; and Hope—a naturalist. These qualities lie within each of you. Rely on these talents, but more importantly, rely on each other. All it takes is the ability to open your minds and follow the clues that Mother Nature (and I) have provided.

Why am I doing this? I have spent much of my life alone studying Grand Canyon, and it is time for you to experience the things I learned. Have patience. I hope you will find the discovery of a lifetime.

Look, listen, be observers of all things beautiful, scary, and mysterious. Rely on your senses and document your thoughts, as even a seemingly obscure one may be the answer to what you seek.

Let's get going! Your first step is to find my friend Kelly Bartlett. Kelly holds the keys to your exploration. Your hard work will be worth it because the next generation needs to understand the mysteries this treasure holds as much as you do.

I love you all.

Gramps

P.S. There is a quote by the poet Carl Sandburg: "For each man sees himself in the Grand Canyon—each one makes his own canyon before he comes, each one brings and carries away his own canyon." I have no doubt that you will each carry away your own canyon and will be changed forever.

P.P.S. Be safe—you are undertaking a bold journey fraught with uncertainty.

"Whoa, that's deep. A bold journey fraught with uncertainty." Oz held up his hands. "Maybe this is more than we bargained for. I'm just sayin'."

"You know Gramps always had a flair for the dramatic." Gran turned away and wiped the tears from her cheeks. Everything was quiet except the wind blowing off the rim of the canyon.

"So this Kelly Bartlett, do you know who he's talking about, Gran?"

Gran shook her head like she was clearing away a cloud of memories. "Kelly Bartlett? Of course, I've met her many times. Gramps visited with Kelly and her husband every time he came to the canyon. She's a wildlife biologist."

"That would make sense since we're here to see the condors," Kira said. "Do you think that's what he wants us to find?"

"Kira, you already told us where to find them. We could just camp out here on the South Rim and save ourselves a long hike. Mystery solved. We've discovered the great secrets of Grand Canyon," Oz said. He nudged me, "Now can we get something to eat? I'm starving."

"Stop, Oz. This is serious. Gramps said there's treasure down there. There's got to be something else."

Oz took a step forward and waved at the others to follow him. "Then what are we waiting for? We need to find the mysterious Kelly Bartlett, but can we get rid of these backpacks first?"

We checked in at the Thunderbird Lodge where we would spend our first night.

"Of course, Gramps picked the Thunderbird Lodge,"

Kira straightened her purple glasses. "In American Indian legends, the thunderbird was an enormous black bird that created thunder and lightning with a flap of its wings. Since condors are the largest birds in North America, Gramps and I always thought the thunderbird legends were about them."

Oz and I dropped our stuff on the floor of the room we were sharing and headed out front to meet the others. The girls and Gran came out fifteen minutes later.

"Isn't it great that we have our own rooms?" Kira said and pulled her long brown hair into a pony tail.

Oz scrunched his eyebrows. "Big deal, Nate and I have our own rooms at home."

"I think Kira is talking about not sharing a room with me," Gran said. "I decided you were all old enough to stay in motel rooms by yourselves. Besides, I heard one of you boys snoring when you stayed at our house once."

Oz and I pointed at each other.

"Hey, Nate. You said on the train that you had a schedule. Can you show it to us?" Hope asked.

The top of Hope's head only came to my chin, so she stood on her tip-toes to read the list over my shoulder.

DAY 1: Arrive at South Rim by train. Stay at Thunderbird Lodge on South Rim
DAY 2: Trans-Canyon shuttle to North Rim. Camp at North Rim Campground
DAY 3: Hike North Kaibab Trail from North Rim Campground to Cottonwood Campground
DAY 4: Second night at Cottonwood Campground
DAY 5: Hike to Bright Angel Campground

DAY 6: Explore Phantom Ranch. Second night at Bright Angel Campground.

DAY 7: Hike on Bright Angel Trail to Indian Garden Campground

DAY 8: Second night at Indian Garden Campground

DAY 9: Hike to South Rim on Bright Angel Trail and leave for home

"Kira and I got online on February 20, to make sure we were some of the first to submit our backcountry permit requests for these sites. The canyon gets really busy in the spring, and you have to reserve all your spots ahead of time."

"I'm tired already and we haven't even started," said Oz.

"Not me. I'm dying to get on the trail," I said.

"Slow down, Nate," Kira said. "There's so much cool stuff we can do on this side before we start our hike."

Kira was right. We had planned to spend the day exploring the South Rim, but first we needed to find Kelly Bartlett.

We hopped on the Grand Canyon shuttle, which dropped us off in front of a huge building: Grand Canyon Visitor Center. At the information desk, we asked for Kelly Bartlett. The ranger on duty peered at us over the counter.

"You just missed her. She went to lunch. Is there something I can help you with?"

"Do you know when she'll be back?" I asked.

"I was surprised to see her up here today because her office is in another building. She's been hovering around the visitor center all morning like she was waiting for somebody. Is it you?"

"Maybe."

"Why don't you look around, and I'll tell her to find you when she returns."

There were tons of people in the visitor center and a lot who were speaking in different languages. We watched the free movie: *Grand Canyon: A Journey of Wonder*. It was pretty amazing to see exactly where we'd be walking for the next week. Kira and I picked up a bunch of Junior Ranger activity booklets: Junior Paleontologist, Night Explorer, and information on becoming a Phantom Rattler Ranger. You could earn one of those badges for getting to the bottom and back up again, which is exactly what we were going to do.

"Why do they call it a Phantom Rattler Ranger? I've seen enough rattlesnakes for a lifetime near my house in Supai," said Hope.

"Not everyone who heads into the canyon sees a rattlesnake, but you might hear one." A woman about my mom's age stood next to me. Her eyes crinkled up when she talked. "You must be Paul Wilder's family."

"And friends," Oz said.

"I'm Kelly Bartlett. I heard you were looking for me." Kelly spotted Gran and ran over to hug her. I had so many questions for her, but I was afraid I would forget something so I started a list on a new page in my notebook. The ladies finished talking, and Kelly led us into an office with a large table. Lying in the middle of it was a thick yellow envelope.

"I've heard all about you from your grandfather. He was a great man and knew so much about the birds here at Grand Canyon. How can I help you?" Kelly said.

I opened my notebook, but Kira spoke first. "Why did

15

Gramps send us to you?"

"I'm not exactly sure. Your grandfather let me know that you would be arriving at the canyon today. He mailed me this envelope several months ago and asked me to give it to you if he couldn't be here. I wish I knew more, but hopefully this will help."

She gave the envelope to Hope, who was sitting beside her, and Hope slid it over to me. I tore it open and found a stack of smaller envelopes. They were all sealed and labeled: #1, #2, #3, #4, #5, #6, #7, and #8 in Gramps' handwriting. I unfolded a loose sheet of paper and read out loud:

Dear Kids,

If you are reading this, you found Kelly. Congratulations! I knew you would be good at this. Enclosed are eight clues to help you in your search. My favorite part of camping was the conversations we had while gathered around the campfire at night. You won't be having campfires in Grand Canyon (except maybe at the North Rim Campground), but that doesn't mean you can't have evening chats. That's why I've given you a clue to open each night of your adventure.

After years of scientific research, I've learned that mysteries are not solved immediately. At first, there will be many questions, and you may feel as though you have no answers. But, don't give up. The solution to one clue is not dependent on your other answers until the end of the hunt. Only then, will everything fit together and lead you to the treasure.

Below you'll find your first clue.

Love, Gramps

Ng A (iii)(vi). (ii)´ (ii)(o).(vii)(ix)(vi)″ ↵ (i)(i)(ii)
(iv)´ (i)(vii).(ii)(ix)(ix)″,

Ibhe frnepu jVYY ortva,
sbe n pevzfba oneevre gung Ibh'YY frr jura
Ibh'er cnfg gur Jngnubzvtv bs gur Fhcnv
naq gur fubpxvat pbzcbfVgr nyfb arneol.

"That's not a clue," Kira said. "It's gibberish. How're we ever supposed to figure it out?"

I STARED AT THE LETTERS in front of me and wondered if Gran or Kelly knew anything about the clues.

I slid the paper across the table to them. "Did Gramps tell you about this?"

Both Gran and Kelly shook their heads.

They handed it to Oz. "Looking at this makes me dizzy," he said and crossed his eyes.

"These must be Roman numerals, right?" I pointed to the Is and Xs in the parentheses. "Together we should be able to figure those out."

I turned to a new page in my notebook and wrote out the Roman numerals with their corresponding numbers below:

A (III)(VI). (II)' (II)(0).(VII)(IX)(VI)" J (I)(I)(II) (IV)' (I) (VIII).(II)(IX)(IX)"

A36 2' 20.796"; J112 4' 18.299"

"Big long numbers with decimals. Is this going to be a quiz, because I didn't sign up for a week of math quizzes.

And what do A and J stand for?" Oz asked.

I thought about the cartography class I took online during the school year. These were much more than decimals. I spread one of my waterproof maps out on the table. It was filled with white and green shaded areas. Curvy lines ran all over the map. The whole thing was covered by a black grid.

Hope leaned in next to me. "What's that?"

"It's a topographic map of Grand Canyon. The curvy lines show the contours of the earth. It's like looking at a 3-D map on a two-dimensional surface. When the lines are far apart, it means the ground is wide open and level, and when they are close together, like this, it means that the land is much steeper."

Hope leaned toward the lower left side of the map and circled the word, 'Havasupai.' "Here's my house, right here in Supai."

"And check out this grid—"

"Wait, you live in Grand Canyon? I thought you lived in California with Kira." Oz interrupted.

"She does, but did you think she just appeared out of nowhere? She has parents and a family, you know," Kira said.

"Well, actually I didn't know, and I was trying to be polite by not prying. Nate is always telling me I'm too nosy. And the one time I try to be—"

"I grew up in Supai, but I tested into a school in California when I was nine. That's when I moved in with Kira's family. Our dads were friends in college," Hope said quietly.

"A school for smart kids, right?" Oz snatched Kira's glasses and perched them on his nose.

Both girls blushed.

"Now I see why Nate is always calling you nosy, Oz. Can we get back to work?" Gran asked.

Oz put his hands up in surrender. "I'm all about work."

"The grid on this map shows GPS coordinates and the numbers in the clue look like they're formatted the same." I showed them how the numbers were divided into two digits representing the degree of latitude or longitude, two more digits representing the minutes and the seconds on the map.

"I've never quite understood how a map can tell time," said Kira.

"It doesn't matter right now. The point is, I think if we follow these coordinates, they'll take us somewhere in Grand Canyon." I traced down the left side of the map to 36 degrees and then up from the bottom at 112 degrees. My fingers met in the middle of the map at the South Rim.

"So you're saying that it's not A and J. It's N and W for North and West?" Kira asked. With that, she was off and running. "If A = N and J = W…"

She grabbed for my notebook, but I was already writing the alphabet on the page. I put the corresponding letters below.

A B C D E F G H I J K L M N O P Q R S T U V W X Y Z
N O P Q R S T U V W X Y Z A B C D E F G H I J K L M

"How did you know it would work that way?" Hope said.

"Just a hunch. I have this book about codes and ciphers. This is a 'Caesar Cipher.' It's the simplest of all ciphers. I knew if A and W fit, then the rest of the alphabet would too."

I filled in the rest of the words using the code. We were left with:

At N 36 2' 20.796", W 112 4' 18.299",
your search will begin,
for a crimson barrier that you'll see when
you're past the Watahomigi of the Supai
and the shocking composite also nearby.

I read the clue three times. "Oz, I guess your cell phone is going to come in handy after all. Let's figure out exactly where these coordinates lead."

"I think I might be able to help," Kelly said. She left the room and came back a few minutes later with a paper in her hand titled, *The Story of the Grand Canyon: A Virtual Caching Activity.*

"Virtual caching is a GPS treasure hunt. You type in coordinates, go to a location, and then figure out a clue that leads you to the next location." Kelly laid the paper in front of us. "The coordinates from your grandfather seem to match those for the beginning of the canyon's caching activity."

Oz's GPS app led us to Yavapai Point, where we found the Yavapai Geology Museum. From the geology museum entrance, we navigated to the first virtual cache. We walked on the edge of the Rim Trail, which dropped off into the canyon below us, until we reached the first sign: "Congratulations! You have just walked the Trail of Time, a geology timeline. You have covered 2 billion years of Grand Canyon history."

"I don't get it. How could we have finished the Trail? We

just started," said Oz.

I glanced at the map. A dotted red line followed the rim of the canyon all the way to a place called Maricopa Point.

At the beginning of the paved trail was a brownish-gold rock with layers of stripes running through it. It sat on a granite base with the words 'Trail of Time' etched into it.

"'Toroweap Sandstone–273 million years old,'" I read on the next stone, which was tannish-red and looked like it had been cracked off of a larger rock.

"'Espalande Sandstone–285 million years old.' It's like traveling backwards in a geological time machine. Every four feet we walk is taking us another million years back in time." I walked past the next stone.

"Geological time machine? That sounds right up your alley, Nate," said Gran.

"This one doesn't just say Esplanade Sandstone, it says 'Supai Group.'" Hope pointed to the word at the top of the base.

"Supai? Like in the clue. And like you, the Havasupai." Oz's green eyes lit up like someone had shined a flashlight into them. "So, Hope, you should know about all of this stuff if you are part of the Supai Group."

"Oz, I think the Supai Group of rocks is just named for the Havasupai Tribe," Kira said. "Hope isn't automatically a geologist because something is named after her people. You're named after a kid's movie, and I don't think you know how the monkeys manage to fly in Oz."

Oz thought for minute. "Good point."

We moved to the next rock labeled: Supai Group: Wescogame Conglomerate.

"Wasn't that the word in the clue? Conglomerate?" Kira asked.

I re-read the clue. "No, 'composite.'"

"Isn't that the same thing? 'Conglomerate' and 'composite.' They both mean 'groups of similar things,' so we must be getting close." Kira walked faster along the trail. At the next stone, she sat down. "Told you. 'Watahomigi' limestone—just like the clue says."

"Watahomigi is my uncle's last name. He's the leader of our tribal council. But his name has an 'e' on the end," Hope said in a soft voice.

"Don't be shy about this. You're like a famous rock star when it comes to geological history here." Oz patted Hope on the back.

"Let's find the next one." My heart was beating fast. I felt like Sherlock Holmes when all of the clues fall into place and he knows he can solve the mystery. I shuffled up to a pinkish-red rock that looked like a hundred pebbles glued together.

"Surprise Canyon Conglomerate–320 million years old. This is it. 'Surprise Canyon' could definitely be the same thing as 'shocking composite.' Listen." I read from the clue.

"'...past the Watahomigi of the Supai and the shocking composite also nearby.' Now we're looking for a 'crimson barrier,'" I checked the wall that separated us from the edge of the canyon to see if it was red, but it was the color of dishwater. "Look around for a 'crimson barrier.'"

Kira walked ahead. "Nate, bring your notebook over here."

There was a rock almost the same color gray as the wall. Its edges, where it had broken off from the rest of a slab, were an orangey-red. "Redwall limestone–340 million years old."

"Get it? 'Redwall' and 'crimson barrier.' This has to be it," Kira said.

I recopied the clue word for word. Beneath it I wrote: Redwall limestone–340 million years old.

"But what does it mean?" Oz walked in a full circle around us. "Did Gramps put another clue around here?"

"No, and we can't open the next one until tonight."

We crawled and ducked under the trees behind the Redwall Limestone, but found nothing. I wrote three pages of notes about twisted branches, and I even drew pictures of what I saw in the distance. A brown lizard skittered down the paved trail, and I decided maybe we should follow it.

"Oz, how about the next GPS coordinate?"

Oz saluted. "Aye, aye, Captain." He typed the next set of numbers into his phone. "Stay steady, straight ahead."

We walked to the second earth cache site, but there was no more information about Redwall Limestone. I consulted the sheet that Kelly Bartlett had given us.

"Lemme see your phone, Oz. Are you sure you typed the second set in correctly?"

Oz handed it to me. "Are you doubting my navigational skills?"

The numbers on the GPS matched the coordinates on the park brochure. I typed in the set for the next stop. "We must be missing something," I said.

Halfway to location number three, Kira stopped at a sign with an arrow pointing to a dirt path. "It's the Bright Angel Trail. We're walking back up this at the end of the week. Let's check it out."

We were so excited to find a landmark that was part of our planned itinerary. We took the sharp right turn shaded by a canopy of trees and jogged down the dirt trail. The path was so crowded we were forced to slow down and walk single file. Ahead of us were people Gran's age, little kids, and even a few guys wearing flip flops who were taking pictures.

I was in front of Kira, and the rest of our group followed along like baby ducks behind us.

"Did you see that lady wearing high heels?" Kira whispered.

"Just be glad we have on our hiking boots," Gran said. "But remember we didn't bring water bottles and trekking poles, so we can't go too far down the trail."

We eased out of line at the first landmark, a carved stone arch above the trail. I rubbed my hand along its sand-papery walls. "Gran's right. We don't want to be anywhere for long without water during the hottest time of the day. Right, Oz?" I peered over my shoulder and expected to see Oz's Chicago Cubs hat above Hope's head.

I must have looked surprised because Kira, Hope, and Gran turned to look behind us.

"Where did Oz go?" Kira stepped past me and stared toward the Rim Trail.

I followed her gaze and saw lots of people, but no Oz.

A family came through the tunnel and as they passed us, the little girl said, "Mommy, did some kid really fall over the wall?"

"Oh, I don't think so, Honey. It's just that someone found a baseball cap dangling over the edge," her mother said. My heart skipped a beat.

"Excuse me. Did you say that someone fell over the wall?"
I asked.

The woman nodded.

"Did you see it happen?" I suddenly felt cold even
though it must have been ninety degrees.

"No, but I did see a ranger holding a hat. It was blue
with a red C on it. Someone also said they thought they saw
a kid climbing out on the ledge up the trail. Maybe he was
looking for his hat," she answered.

A blue hat with a red C? That was the Chicago Cubs
logo. I swallowed hard and grabbed Gran's arm, but she already had her cell phone out.

"When did you last see him?" She turned to Hope, who
had been at the back of the pack.

Hope's face went white. "I don't know. Nate took off

26

so fast down the trail. I was just trying to keep up with you guys."

Gran took a deep breath. "I'm sure he's fine. Probably just stopped to ask someone a question. You know that Oz makes friends wherever he goes. I'll call him." Gran punched the buttons on her phone.

A deep voice saying, "I am Oz, the Great and Powerful," echoed off the canyon wall. We all jumped.

The voice repeated, and I ran back up the trail to see where the *Wizard of Oz* ringtone was coming from. No matter how far I moved, the voice wasn't getting any quieter. I stopped and dug around in my daypack, but found nothing. Then I realized it was blasting from the pocket of my shorts. Oz had given me his phone on the Trail of Time to check the GPS coordinates.

The girls caught up, and we found the ledge that the lady described. The drop off was steep and covered with loose rock. We sprinted the rest of the way back to the rim, pushing our way through crowds of people. I didn't see Oz anywhere.

In front of us, a ranger stood with five people crowded around all talking at once. He held a cell phone to his ear. Was he talking to other rangers or the police? Was my best friend missing or maybe...

I TUGGED ON THE RANGER'S ARM like a four-year old. "Have you seen a red-haired kid? About this tall?" I leveled my hand near my shoulder. The ranger held up his finger and pointed to his cell phone. I questioned the people gathered around him.

"He's wearing a blue t-shirt?" No one had seen him.

The ranger didn't seem like he was in a hurry to get off the phone, so we ran up the paved path to the Kolb Studio on the Rim Trail. Gran and Hope said they would check inside. Kira and I dashed ahead to the Lookout Studio. We both froze in our tracks when we saw another ranger on the path. He held a Cubs baseball hat.

"There have to be lots of people with Cubs hats." Kira's voice quivered.

Of course, she was right, but I just knew the hat was Oz's.

"Excuse me," I said to the ranger.

"Oh, is this yours?" he asked.

"No, but it looks like my friend's."

"Is his name Oz?"

I couldn't breathe, let alone answer him. How did he know that? The ranger turned the hat inside out and showed me the scrawled black letters that said: OZ FOREMAN.

Gran and Hope appeared at our sides.

Kira nodded to the ranger. "He's our friend. But people were saying that…"

He chuckled. "I heard that rumor too. It was only a rumor, though."

At that moment, I heard a familiar voice: "Naaaaaate." Running toward us, his hands full of dripping ice cream cones, was Oz, the great and powerful.

"Where have you been?" I yelled and rushed to his side.

"At the Bright Angel Lodge getting ice cream. I wanted to surprise you, but it took you so long to get back up here. And it's like being in an oven out here. It all melted." He held up five empty ice cream cones.

I punched him in the arm. "You can't do that. Ever again. They said that you fell over the ledge. I was picturing you dead on some rock."

"Geez. You're like my mom. You worry too much." Oz pushed me back with his sticky hands.

The ranger held out the hat. "Is this yours?" Oz's face turned red and he nodded.

"How did you get—"

"Oz," Gran snatched the hat from the ranger. "You scared us. People have been looking for you. Rule number one of this trip is that we stick together."

Oz looked at the ground. "I should have told you where I was going. I didn't think it would take long, and when the wind blew my hat away, I figured one of you guys would pick it up. I'm sorry," he said quietly.

"I'm just glad you're okay. What would I do without the Great and Powerful Oz?" I waved his cell phone in front of his face, but he shook his head.

"No, I can't take it now. Look at my hands." His shirt, arms, and hands were covered in pink and brown drips.

"And you smell like sour milk."

Oz lifted his shirt to his nose. "Yeah, maybe I do."

Gran placed the cones in a trash can nearby. "It was a nice thought, Oz, but please don't do that again. And now, you need a shower. Guess we should head back to the lodge."

"I'm sorry, Gran. Just so you know, that ice cream was the best I've ever tasted. That's the first thing I'm getting at the end of our hike," he said.

We hadn't even begun our journey into Grand Canyon, and we'd already lost someone. After Oz showered and our heart rates returned to normal, we went to dinner at the Bright Angel Lodge Cafe next door to our hotel. We all ordered giant cheeseburgers.

"Should we open the next clue now?" I said, while we waited for our food.

Everyone nodded.

"Didn't you leave it in our room?" Oz asked.

"Nope." I picked up my notebook from the floor next to my chair and took out the envelope marked #2. I was relieved we didn't have to take the time to decipher a code.

Along the South Rim Trail and near a Spanish inn, find a heart-shaped stone, let your quest begin.

Above the canyon floor, reaching toward the sky:
temples, pyramids, towers, buttes, above them raptors fly.
From east to west and north to south, look for them each day.
In the end, you'll understand one points the way.

Gran took the note from my hand and mouthed the words to the clue. Her face lit up.

"I know exactly the place," she said.

The waitress set five plates in front of us.

"Can I also order an ice cream sundae?" asked Oz.

"No time for that, Oz. Everyone must eat quickly so we can get to this spot before the sun sets," Gran said.

Oz looked disappointed, but I knew he still felt bad about his disappearing act, and he wouldn't push it with Gran.

I squirted spicy mustard all over my cheeseburger and stuffed it in my mouth. All I could think about was Gramps' poem. I knew it had something to do with rock formations, so I flipped through my notebook and looked for the sketches I drew earlier.

Gran paid the bill, and we headed back to the Rim Trail. She led us to a hotel called the El Tovar, where President Theodore Roosevelt stayed in 1908. This had to be the 'Spanish inn' from Gramps' clue. Gran said it was named after a Spanish explorer, Don Pedro de Tovar, who reported the existence of Grand Canyon to other travelers.

In front of the El Tovar was the wall that overlooked the canyon. Gran laid her hand flat on one its stones. She lifted her fingers. The rock was shaped like a heart.

"Gramps and I loved to come here. They say that one of

31

the workers who built this wall in the 1930s put this heart-shaped stone here for his sweetheart to see."

Normally I would roll my eyes at all that love stuff, but I knew Gramps had led us to this rock for something more important than a sappy story. I sat on a bench made from a huge log. The canyon rock formations stretched as far as I could see and many were similar to the drawings on Gramps' letter.

The rock shapes blended together as the sky darkened. I tried to sketch each one but couldn't get the outlines precise. Instead, I made a list of temples, pyramids, towers, and buttes. I unfolded the map and realized that many were named for Egyptian landmarks and other places in the world:

Buddha Temple
Manu Temple
Zoroaster Temple
Brahma Temple
Deva Temple
Osiris Temple

And that was just the temples. There were also dozens of pyramids, like Cheops Pyramid. Towers: Tower of Ra, Tower of Set. Buttes: Howlands and O'Neill. How were we ever going to figure out which one pointed the way?

Hope sat down next to me. "What're you doing?"

"I'm making a lists of all the rock formations, so we can narrow down the choices."

She looked quietly at my list. "That's a lot of choices," she said. "What's this?" She pointed to the sketches on the side of my notebook.

"I was trying to draw some of them, hoping the pictures might help later."

"Can I try?" Hope held out her hand, and I gave her my pencil. Her fingers moved quickly, while she stared out toward the canyon. Even though the sun would set soon, I could see that her contours followed the rocks exactly.

"How do you tell them apart?" I asked.

"What?"

"The rocks; they all look the same to me." I put my finger on one in the notebook with two triangle shapes connected by a flat portion. "Where is that one?"

Hope pointed to her left about halfway to the first big chasm. It all blurred together: layer after layer of rock.

"It still all looks the same."

"Squint your eyes. That's what I do. Then your mind can see the outlines. When you open your eyes wide again, you can focus on individual ones."

I tried it. The formation Hope pointed to came into perfect focus.

Kira plopped down next to me on the bench. She watched me squinting my eyes.

"What are you doing? Do you need glasses, Nate?"

Hope and I laughed. "Nah, just something Hope taught me. I'm making a list of all the rock formations so that we can figure out which one points the way."

"What about over there?" Kira pointed to a formation right on the edge of the rim.

"According to the map, it's called Battleship Mesa."

"That's Battleship Mesa? No wonder the ranger was

looking for condors there this morning. A nesting pair has returned to it for the last three years. And Gramps even said, 'above them raptors fly.' Those raptors have to be condors." She wrote Battleship Mesa on my list.

"But it's a 'mesa,' and Gramps specifically said, 'pyramid, temples, tower, and buttes.' Besides, I don't think it's going to be that easy for us figure out the answer, Kira."

I decided to change the subject. I turned to Hope.

"It's amazing that you can see the outlines so clearly. How'd you learn to do that?"

Hope rubbed the brown woven bracelet she wore on her right arm.

"When I was a kid, I spent a lot of time looking at these spires at the end of the valley near my house." Hope reached into her pocket and unfolded a scratched-up photo. The picture showed a bright blue sky with a red rock wall like the ones in the canyon and two stone towers rising from it.

"These are the 'wigleeva,' the guardian spirits of Supai. Our tribe has a legend that says that if these spires ever fall, the walls of the canyon will close in on the Havasupai people and destroy them." Hope's shiny black hair covered her face as she looked down at the photo. "When I was a kid, I used to stare at their outlines. I memorized every curve and notch because I was terrified that they would crumble and the guardians would abandon us and our home."

"That's horrible," I said.

"Legends aren't supposed to be happy. They explain the unexplainable. I always liked the idea of them watching over me," she said.

"Sure, until they fall down and the walls close in on everyone." I shivered. I thought about Hope's words—explain the unexplainable. We had spent the last twenty-fours with a lot more unexplainable questions than answers. Then it dawned on me.

"Maybe we need something to tell *our* story in the canyon, like a legend. A legend about our adventures, but of course, with a happy ending."

"DO LEGENDS HAVE HEROES?
Because I'm definitely the hero of this group. And Kira
could be the evil scientist in a lab coat and spectacles." Oz
looked over the seat of the van at Kira who stuck her tongue
out at him.

"It's not a comic book, Oz. It's a legend. It's more about
symbols than cartoon characters. It's just a way to tell our
story," I said.

"Fine, but let's not put anything about me being lost or
everyone thinking I was dead, okay? My mom is going to be
mad enough when she hears I wandered off. No reason to
remind her in our super hero legend, is there?"

"It's not about super heroes," we all said at once. The
rest of the people in the van turned to look at us. We were
rolling along in the 16-passenger Trans-Canyon shuttle: me,
Kira, Oz, Hope, Gran, our driver, and two groups of hikers.
One group seemed like they were my parents' age and the
others were three guys who had torn shirts and smelled like
the locker room after gym class. We had loaded our gear at
8 a.m. sharp and settled in for the four-and-a-half-hour ride

to the North Rim.

The distance we would hike between the North Rim and the South Rim was only 23.9 miles, but it takes 4.5 hours to drive from one rim to the other. You have to go all the way around the outside of the canyon.

When we left the South Rim Village, we were suddenly on regular highways with miles of scrub brush and desert rocks, and we couldn't see the canyon at all.

Kira and I sat next to each other and reviewed our hiking guides and itinerary. One of the stinky guys named Todd sat next to me.

"Are you guys doing a day hike from the rim or what?" he asked.

"No, we're hiking rim-to-rim. We'll arrive back at the South Rim seven days from now. How 'bout you?" I said.

"Really? The five of you are hiking rim-to-rim." He circled his fingers around our group, "How old are you? Like, fourteen?"

"Nope. We're all twelve, and she's…" I pointed at Gran. She turned around quickly. "I'm twelve… and then some." We all laughed. Todd took a swig of water.

"That's pretty awesome that you guys are doing that. Great idea to take your time, too. We've done rim-to-rim hikes twice, but we're heading down Nankoweap Trail this time."

I'd read about Nankoweap Trail. It was probably the hardest trail in the canyon. Gran might be able to do it, but none of us could…yet.

"You'll have the best time. Just be sure you don't get dehydrated, and watch out for rattlesnakes," Todd said.

Hope leaned over the seat. She had been reading for

more than an hour. "Seriously. I really don't like rattlesnakes."

"Nah, I'm kidding. You'll be fine. Just keep your eyes and ears open," said Todd.

Oz slid over closer to Hope. "What do you have against snakes? Has one ever zapped you?" Oz pinched Hope's arm and laughed.

"Cut it out, Oz," I said.

Kira slapped the back of Oz's head. "Yeah, quit being such a brat."

Hope sighed. "It's okay. It's just that a snake bit one of my cousins and she was pretty sick for a while."

"Sorry," Oz said. "I was just fooling around. So, on a more intellectual note. You've been reading since we got into the van. I get sick if I even open a book in the car." Oz pounded the screen of his phone with his finger.

"But it looks like you can play video games with no problem. Do you do anything except obsess over that phone?" asked Kira.

Oz twisted around in his seat. "Sure, I go on long walks every day with these two." He put his arm around Gran and pointed at me. "And I watch a lot of 'Wildman' on TV."

"'Wildman'? I don't even know what that is," Hope said.

"Dude, I love that show," stinky Todd said. "I can't tell you how many things I've learned from him that I've used in the backcountry. Never anything super serious like drinking your own pee, but lots of other outdoor survival stuff."

"I know. He's the best, right? See, Kira, I do have some skills. Even our new friend Todd says the hours I've spent with Wildman will make me a useful backcountry companion." Oz smiled and went back to poking his phone screen.

"You're my best friend, Oz. But I'm not drinking my own pee, no matter what you say."

About that time, the van pulled off for our first pit stop at Cameron, Arizona. The Cameron Trading Post looked like something out of an Old West movie, and the sign said it was built in 1916.

"A trading post?" Oz asked. "We're in the middle of nowhere. Who would be coming here to trade things?"

"That's the point, Oz. People lived so far apart and the American Indians used this as a meeting place and brought their livestock and homemade blankets to trade for supplies and food that they couldn't grow themselves," Gran said.

As we walked inside, I pointed to a room filled with woven blankets. They had complicated designs in red, black, and gold.

"Like these?" I asked.

"That's right, Nate," Gran said. "Those are actually rugs, not blankets, but were most likely made by the Navajo Tribe. Even today, the owners of the trading post still buy handmade art from tribes all over the area."

The gift shop was filled with baskets, pottery, and cases of silver jewelry. I pointed to a bracelet in one of the displays.

"Is this like yours, Hope?" She eyed it carefully and then held out her arm with the bracelet she was always twirling around her wrist.

"No, that looks like it's Navajo or Zuni. See these?" Aqua-colored stones filled the bracelet. "Those tribes use a lot of turquoise in their jewelry. Mine is just braided fibers."

I wondered where Hope got her bracelet, but before I

could ask her, the van driver said we needed to leave. I was sad we had to go. I wanted to look for the dinosaur tracks Gran said were in the sandstone used to build the walls of the trading post art gallery.

Two hours later, we finished our second stop at Marble Canyon. Huge red cliffs rose from the ground to our right.

"Keep your eyes open," Kira said. "This is the exact area where they release the condors every year."

"You're right, Kira," said Gran. "Young condors that have been bred in captivity are released by the Peregrine Fund every year. You never know, we might see some today."

I didn't see anything except soaring rock walls. Kira held her binoculars to her eyes and scanned the skies.

"Holy guacamole!" Kira screamed and bounced in her seat.

"What going on?" asked Oz.

"Way out there...look...two condors are circling."

I peered over her and spotted two black birds in the distance. "How do you know they aren't turkey vultures? I read that turkey vultures look just like condors."

"You don't even know what you're talking about, Nate."

"You don't either. You told me you've never seen one in real life."

Kira slammed the binoculars into my stomach. "Look. See how they hold their wings flat and fly straight like they are gliding on an invisible sheet of ice. Turkey vultures hold their wings slightly up in a V shape, and they wobble back and forth in the wind."

I watched the birds soar for a minute. "Those guys definitely don't look wobbly."

"And if they were closer, you'd be able to see patches of white feathers on the underside of their wings. But since they're faraway, the flight pattern is how you know."

"How do you know all this?" I asked.

"Gramps taught me about them when I was working on my project."

The condors finally disappeared in the distance. I handed the binoculars back to Kira, and she sighed. "That might be the only time I ever see one."

The van drove down a smaller road where pine trees grew on both sides. It was like entering another world, from desert to forest in one second. We passed a sign for Little Park Lake and then a herd of bison. At a clearing that looked like it should have been filled with trees, the ground was covered in dead trunks—like a box of giant toothpicks spilled all over the earth.

"What happened to the forest?" Oz asked.

"Looks like a wildfire," said Gran.

Our driver cleared his throat. "You're right. This area is part of the Kaibab National Forest. In 2012, there was a 105-acre fire caused by lightning. The whole area was blanketed in smoke. The Forest Service also conducts prescribed burns once in a while to get rid of dead trees."

"You know about plants and trees, Gran. Aren't fires the worst thing that could happen in a place like this?" I asked. We don't worry much about wildfires in Chicago.

"It's part of the natural process of the forest ecosystem. Fire clears out the dense, overcrowded forests and allows new tree growth. It looks devastating, but it's the way the forest regenerates."

Gramps and Kira weren't the only scientists in our family. Gran was a research botanist before she retired.

At the North Rim Entrance Station, the ranger on duty waved us through. We were back in Grand Canyon National Park. The van stopped in front of the North Rim General Store. It looked similar to the train depot on the South Rim, but much smaller and with a covered porch on the front. We unloaded our gear from the back of the van.

"So long, young dudes and dudettes. We're hitting the trail today. I hope you have the greatest hike ever. You'll always remember your first rim-to-rim. Keep on trekkin'."

Todd gave us a salute, threw his pack on his back, and started off down the road. His friends followed him, and they disappeared into the forest.

The five of us huddled and I laid out our plan.

"Okay, we need to check in at the campground registration building, pick up our permits at the Backcountry Information Center, and set up camp." I felt like a drill sergeant giving orders. "Gran, Hope, and Oz, can you figure out the campsite stuff? Kira and I will get our backcountry permits, and we'll be there to help set up the tents."

"Yes, sir." Oz saluted just like Todd had.

"Just a minute, Nate. I should probably go with you to the Backcountry Information Center. They might question two twelve-year-olds checking in on their own. I know that you are fully capable, but the park service probably won't be thrilled with two unaccompanied minors heading down the trail. We have all day. Let's do this together." Gran hugged me. I knew she was right, but I still hated that we needed an adult to do everything.

"Okay. Let's all set up camp and then find the Back-country Office."

The first thing I noticed was how much cooler it was on the North Rim. Ponderosa pines shaded the camping sites, and a breeze blew constantly. When I bent down to pick up my pack, I got a whiff of pine needles. It was exactly as I imagined the forest of Narnia in *The Lion, the Witch, and the Wardrobe*. There were two other groups in line at the campground registration cabin, so three of us leaned against a tall tree, while Gran worked her way up to the window. Oz was trying to get one of the camper's dogs to fetch a stick he was throwing.

I couldn't stop thinking about the legend—our legend—and how it might lead us to the answers we were looking for. Seeing those condors seemed like it was an important part of the trip, so I turned to a new page in my notebook. Kira leaned close to me and read the words as I wrote them.

When the elder was near the end of his life, he spoke to his people. He said it was time for them to journey into the great canyon to learn about its mysteries. The elder's riddles would guide their path, but only through patience would they discover the answers.

They listened to his words and wished the elder could be with them. When a giant bird circled near the bright red cliffs, they felt he was. For the bird was a thunderbird, like the ones the elder observed for so many years.

"This is good. Especially the part about the thunder-birds. Could we take turns writing parts of the legend?"

Before I could answer, a rattle drifted up from the scrub grass next to us. The blades shook. I froze. Kara grabbed my arm, and Hope backed away.

"I told you guys how much I hate rattlesnakes."

WE ALL LEAPED IN DIFFERENT
directions away from the sound. The more I listened, the
more I was convinced it wasn't a rattlesnake. Not that I
would know since I've only listened to recordings of them
online, but the noise didn't sound as scary. Then a furry
white tail appeared. I may not be an expert, but I know
snakes don't have tails like stuffed animals.

The blades of grass continued to shake until Oz arrived
with his stick. Out popped a gray squirrel with a rust-col-
ored stripe on its back and that white tail. Its ears were
pointed and the hair on the tips stood up like the squirrel
had the worst case of bed head ever. It watched us.

"I just saw one of those little guys over there, too," Oz
said. "What kind of mutant squirrel is it? And Hope, you
look like you saw a ghost. Oh, did you think it was a you-
know-what?"

She nodded. "I don't know what kind of squirrel it is. We
don't have those in Supai."

"That's a Kaibab squirrel. The North Rim is the only
place in the world you can find them. I know about their

feeding habits too." Kira put her glasses on and watched the squirrel dart in and out of the trees and long grass. "They mark the trees where they eat so they can find the same ones again. Something about the nutritional components of those particular—"

"Really, Kira. Could you be any more of a nerd?" Oz asked.

Kira took her glasses off and shoved them in her backpack. She stormed off toward Gran. Hope and I both looked at Oz.

"What?" He held up both hands. "You know it's true. But," Oz yelled in the direction of Kira, "you're the coolest nerd I know."

I caught up with Kira, and distracted her with finding our campsite on the map. We reserved it more than a year in advance because we knew it would get taken quickly. Trees surrounded it, except on the canyon side, where it opened up with steep drop offs.

Hope and Oz followed us to our spot and were both impressed.

"Boy am I glad I don't sleepwalk. One wrong step in the middle of the night, and you'd be flying through the air… down there."

Kira laughed. I was happy that Oz's nerd comments weren't bugging her anymore.

Once Gran joined us, we got to work setting up camp. First, tents: one for Gran, one for the boys, and one for the girls. Gran carried her own tent, and Oz and I lost the coin toss, so we each had a tent in our packs, too. Oz and I practiced setting up the tent in my backyard before we left, so we finished fast and helped Gran. Our campsite was big enough for all three of our two-person tents. Gran and I got some wood from the camp host and set up a campfire for later—our last night in civilization.

When we picked up our permit at the Backcountry Office for the rest of our trip, the ranger looked at our itinerary and maps. She also gave us information about water and natural springs in the areas we would be hiking.

"Be careful out there," the ranger said. "Stay hydrated. Even in the spring, it gets hot once you're into the canyon. It will be even hotter at Phantom Ranch. And be sure to take advantage of the Ranger activities there."

"Um…I have a question." Oz looked at the ground and smiled in a way I'd never seen before. "Will I have a cell signal down there? My mom told me to ask." We all groaned.

The ranger laughed. "Believe it or not, you aren't the first person to ask me that. You might have a signal for parts of the trip, but don't rely on your phone as a communication tool. Plus, the canyon is one of the best places in the world for you to 'unplug.'" She made her fingers into air quotes and smiled at Oz.

"It's only seven days, Oz," said Kira.

When we got back to camp, Hope sat down to write. I assumed it was another letter to her grandmother. Oz wandered off, and Kira and I sat at the picnic table and read a brochure the ranger had given us: "10 Summer Hiking Essentials." It was only May 20th, so not summer yet, but if Oz's melting ice cream on the South Rim was any indication, we were in for a hot trip.

"Water." I marked on our map all the places the ranger

told us we could load up on water.

"It says 'with electrolyte replacement,'" Kira said. "How much do we have?" I counted out 50 foil packets filled with Gatorade powder.

"I hope that's enough. What's next?"

"Backpack, flashlight with spare batteries, maps, sunscreen, hats."

I tugged the brim of my green fishing hat down over my ears. I looked silly compared to Oz in his baseball cap, but my mom made me bring a hat that would also cover the back of my neck.

"Food," Kira said.

"Yep, plenty of that." I spread out packages of jerky, three plastic jars of peanut butter, crackers, cans of tuna, and Ziplocs filled with dehydrated food.

"That dehydrated stuff sounds gross," Kira said.

"Oz and I tasted it at home. It was like sucking down a mouthful of sawdust. Once we added hot water, it was pretty good though," I said.

"You ate it without adding water?"

"We didn't really read the directions first," I took the list from Kira and tried to move on to the next item.

"You always have to read the instructions." Kira laughed. "Seriously, you guys are so dense."

"That's why we brought you, brainiac. What's next?"

"Signal mirror or whistle," Kira said.

"I have a whistle on my backpack, but I don't think we brought a signal mirror."

Oz walked up. He shook pine needles out of his hair and dumped them out of the hood of his sweatshirt.

"Oh, no worries, mate," Oz said in his best Australian accent. "Wildman taught me this." Oz angled his cell phone at the sun, which was almost to the horizon. He waved it back and forth until a bright light reflected off of the screen and onto Hope's face.

"Hey, stop." Hope shaded her eyes from the bright light.

"In the 'Lost in the Sahara Desert' episode, Wildman said that any reflective piece of metal or glass, like my cell phone screen, can work as a signal mirror if we're lost."

"We don't need a helicopter seeing our signal and coming to rescue us here. But good thinking, Oz." I checked the list for the last item. "I know Gran has the first aid kit, so I think we're set."

Gran must have heard her name because she walked over to the table where we had our supplies spread out. "I'd say we're prepared for almost anything. Right now, though, I think it's time to enjoy one last real meal before we have to tear into our gourmet dehydrated feasts. Are you ready for dinner?"

We repacked our essentials, so Gran could spread out the sandwiches, apples, and cookies from the General Store on the picnic table. The sun was setting, and Gran lit the campfire. The canyon looked like it was on fire, too.

"So awesome, Gran." Oz took a bite from a chocolate chip cookie.

"Hold on there," said Gran. "Nate, as our group leader, do you have any last words of wisdom before we hit the trail tomorrow?"

I didn't know what to say. Kira and I were leading together. She grinned and mouthed 'better you than me.' I picked up the sandwiches, passing them out while I tried to think of something wise to say.

"Um…Gramps said that he has put us on a path of discovery. I hope we all discover something about Grand Canyon and maybe something about ourselves?"

It sounded more like a question than something profound a leader would say, but everyone seemed satisfied. After dinner, Gran walked to the pay phones near the General Store to call our parents and let them know we were safe. The four kids decided to hike on the Transept Trail near the campground, but not before we put on our sweatshirts. The air had turned cool.

"Come on, you guys. The sun is almost gone, and I want to get to Bright Angel Point before it sets," said Kira.

Oz was playing hide and seek with a Kaibab squirrel that jumped between branches on the trees above us. I hung back trying to get a better view of the temples and buttes with Kira's binoculars.

"According to the map, we have to wind into the forest before we curve out to the canyon rim again," said Kira.

Just like she said, the trail turned left and climbed into the forest area. The trees grew closer together and this section of the trail was much darker. Hope stopped to tie her shoe. The orange glow from the canyon was fading to gray.

Hope lifted her head and bit her lip. "Don't anyone move," she whispered. She nodded toward a bush beside me. I twisted my head, and two eyes as big as car headlights stared back at me.

A low growl and then a hiss drifted from the shadows. I reached into my pocket for my flashlight, but never looked away from the unblinking yellow eyes. My fingers closed around the cold metal. I fumbled for the button to turn it on. I looked down for only a second and the animal let out a piercing scream.

"**IS IT A BEAR?**" Oz whispered. "No one said anything about bears."

The bushes shook and the animal screamed again. This time like a little girl screeching.

"That doesn't sound like a bear," Hope said. "It's got to be some kind of big cat."

A shadow moved to a bush close to Kira. She turned and ran back up the trail.

"Kira," I yelled. "Stop. Now! Hold your arms above your head. Everyone else do the same. Make yourselves look big and make a lot of noise."

My heart was beating double-time. "Now everyone, back away but don't run."

We moved in slow motion and yelled. I shined my flashlight around, but the animal's screams sounded farther away.

"Hope was probably right. What you described sounds like a bobcat on its nightly prowl for food," Gran said when we returned to the campsite.

"Just as long as we weren't going to be its dinner." Oz rubbed his hands together.

Gran laughed. "I think it was more scared of your yelling than you were of it."

I looked up bobcats in my Grand Canyon backcountry guide. "It's says very few visitors to the canyon see bobcats."

"I'm fine being part of the group that never sees them," said Kira.

We had been so focused on training for our hike, we hadn't even thought about the animals we might encounter. Unlike Hope, who saw tons in Supai, the three of us mostly saw animals at the zoo.

"Listen to this. It's a recording of a bobcat." Oz held up his phone and the screams were identical to what we had heard.

"But that's just a recording. We were face-to-face with that thing." Kira shivered. "We live in California and don't have screaming bobcats roaming around."

"Actually, you do. I saw a story on the news one time about bobcats. You just don't see them. We have to be prepared to see more animals in the canyon. We can't freak out every time something new shows up," I said.

"Nate's right. We have to be prepared for everything. And that's why I did this." Oz led us over to our tent and unzipped the doors. A layer of pine needles as tall as my hand covered the floor, and our sleeping bags were on top of them.

"What did you do?" I pushed past him.

"Hang on. Dude, Wildman does this all the time. He fills up his parachute with pine needles to sleep on. Sleeping on the ground is cold, and it's cold tonight, right?"

Kira zipped her sweatshirt and Hope tucked her long hair into a stocking hat.

"Wildman is trying to survive in the middle of nowhere. We're in a National Park. You can't move pine needles around."

"But the pine needles trap your body heat. Not only are they soft to lay on, they'll insulate us from the ground. Believe me, Nate. You'll thank me in the morning."

"I'll thank you when you've put all the pine needles back where you found them. Remember that 'Leave No Trace' video we watched on the park service website?"

"Sure. It said don't move around animals and artifacts. These are just pine needles."

"It doesn't matter, Oz. The pine needles are part of the natural environment too. You can't move them," Kira said.

"Put them back so we can open another clue," I said. Oz rolled his eyes and sighed, but picked up handfuls of needles and returned them to the base of the trees. When he finally finished, I tore open the third envelope and read:

> Is nature's soundscape quiet tonight?
> You must listen, but turn off your light
> To hear all the chirpers and screechers;
> There's an abundance of creatures.
> Some are the predators, some are the prey,
> Many you never see in the day.
> Some may be on the threatened list.
> As a pair, can you name those in your midst?

So far, we'd heard: the chattering of the squirrel, the

scream of the bobcat, and all the birds that never seemed to stop singing.

"What is it with the pair? 'As a pair, can you name those in your midst?'" Oz said. "Does he mean that we need to be in pairs or is he talking about pairs of animals?"

"The threatened list, that part's easy. Nate, look in the guidebook. There was a whole list of threatened and endangered species in there. Maybe that's what we're looking for," Kira said.

I found the page and read it to myself.

"There are lots of bats. Maybe we're listening for a bat," I said.

"Do bats even make noise?" Oz asked.

"Northern leopard frog? Southwest river otter? There are twenty-five on this page. This will be a noisy place if all these animals make noise. Plus, it says to turn off our lights. So maybe we need to figure out which of these animals are nocturnal." I yawned and closed the book.

"You are definitely not nocturnal, Nate. How about we go to sleep. We have all day on the trail tomorrow to figure this out," Gran said. She climbed into her tent with her flashlight.

Kira and Hope crawled into their tent, and finally Oz and I were in our sleeping bags.

I turned off my flashlight, but Oz was still busy arranging things. He tucked his whistle into the mesh pocket on the tent wall. He arranged his water bottle near his head, his flashlight between us, and lay down. It was quiet for one minute and then the tent lit up from the light on his phone.

"May 20. North Rim Campground. All is quiet so far tonight. My partner and I are secure in our bivouac…"

Oz pretended to narrate a television show about all of the things in our tent.

"Tonight, we're listening to the soundscape. Hoping to hear a creature…a threatened creature perhaps…who will lead us to our treasure. Shh…let's listen." Oz cupped his ear with his hand and lay frozen in that ridiculous pose.

A sound like a dog's bark pierced the silence. It was probably the puppy that Oz had been playing with earlier. Three quick barks.

Oz jumped and put his arm around me.

"If you don't be quiet, you are going to be on the endangered species list." I laughed, pushed him away, and fell asleep listening to the sounds in the distance.

Oz's phone buzzed at 6 a.m. We wanted to get an early start before the day turned hot. We packed up our camp and waited for the North Rim General Store to open so we could buy fruit and sandwiches for lunch. Our first day on the trail, we'd be hiking 6.8 miles to Cottonwood Campground.

By the time we reached the North Kaibab trailhead, the sun was shining. It was cold, though, so we wore our jackets. My pack weighed 18.5 pounds when we'd hung it on the giant meat hook attached to a scale at the Backcountry Information Center the night before. We didn't have to carry too much water because there was a water filling station at the Supai Tunnel, 1.7 miles down the trail. I still felt like I was carrying a bag filled with boulders on my back.

As we set off on the trail, we passed a sign which Oz read for us in a very serious voice. "When mules are present stand quietly to the side. Follow mule guide's instructions." The ranger at the Backcountry Information Center warned us about the mule trains. If the mules approached, we were supposed to stand on the inside of the trail so we didn't accidentally get knocked off the steep edges. After the mule team passed, we could start hiking again.

"Let's get going." I looked at my watch. "It's 7:15, and the first mule train of the day leaves the North Rim at 7:30. If we move fast, we should be able to stay in front of them."

"Don't you want to see the mules," Oz asked. "I think it sounds cool." Most of the animals we'd seen so far hadn't bothered me, but I wasn't sure I liked the idea of sharing a narrow trail with a mule.

"I just think it would be better to have the trail to ourselves," I said.

Soon we were on a series of switchbacks winding down a steep hill into the canyon. There were cliffs in the distance and lots of different colored rocks: red, brown, white, and green—like a birthday cake with layers. I'd read about all the fossils layered in geological time. It was crazy to imagine how long they'd been there.

I was first in line, with Kira behind me, then Hope, then Oz, and Gran. Oz made a big deal about staying in the back to watch out for Gran. After the incident with the Cubs hat, I think it was really Gran watching out for Oz.

"So," I said after we'd walked in silence for awhile.

"What did we hear last night? Any strange sounds from the soundscape?"

"One of you was snoring in your tent," Kira said. I looked back. Oz pointed at me.

"It was Nate," Oz said. "I can prove it." He pulled his cell phone from his pocket and pushed a button. There was silence and then the sounds of squirrels chirping, followed by a loud honking and sputtering sound.

"What is that?" Kira clapped her hands over her ears.

"It's a recording of the night soundscape. I left it running so that we could capture the 'creatures and screechers.'" Oz looked proud.

"I don't think we need to capture a screecher. It sound like we've got one right here," Gran smiled at Oz.

"That's not me. That's Nate." The snoring noise boomed from the phone.

"No way. I don't snore," I said.

"Dude, I heard you—"

A garbled voice broke into the recording. "I am Oz…" snoring…"the Great and Powerful," followed by a loud snort.

"Sounds like you are the Great and Powerful snorer. That's one to include in our legend."

"Speaking of our legend," Hope stopped to let the dust settle. We walked far apart to avoid kicking up clouds of red dirt, but our clothes were still covered. My socks and shoes were now reddish-brown. Mom would be itching to get the dirt out of my clothes from this trip.

"Can I write some, too?" she asked.

"Sure. What should we include next? The bobcat, the squirrel that scared us?"

The next section of trail flattened out, and we passed through areas of thick brush. I watched every set of bushes carefully because I couldn't quit thinking about the bobcat from the night before. I know that they don't hunt during the day, but I still wanted to be careful.

Near a big rock tucked into a shady area, Kira called for a rest break. I was happy because my feet hurt. Eighteen pounds doesn't sound like much, but imagine strapping two gallons of milk on your back. That's what it felt like. I found a spot off the trail to drop my pack and put my feet up. Gran opened her pack, and pulled out her tent, a sleeping pad and some clothes.

"What's up, Gran. Are you okay?" I took a long drink of water.

"Let this be a packing lesson. Something has been jabbing me in the back all the way down the trail." Her arm appeared from the pack and she held a skinny, silver handle. A stack of metal cooking pots that looked like buckets was in her hand. "This was definitely not in the right place."

The bushes rustled next to me, and I inched toward the side of the trail. A deer, unlike any I'd ever seen, was curled up in the grass. It had tall ears that looked like a rabbit.

Gran peered over my shoulder and smiled. "It's a mule deer. They're really common in the canyon. She may have come up from Roaring Springs, on the other side of Supai Tunnel, in search of shade after getting a drink there."

According to our map, we were almost to the Supai Tunnel, which was going to be our next water stop. The deer watched me with her huge eyes, but didn't seem scared. Suddenly, the quiet of the canyon was broken by the sound of talking and footsteps. A cloud of dust rose from the trail.

"Looks like our break was too long. Here comes the mule train," Kira said.

We had dodged mule bombs (mounds of poop–some just big piles of dried grass and others still wet and greenish) all the way down the trail, but I hoped we would stay ahead of the actual mules.

"Everyone up against the wall on the inside of the trail." Gran's voice sounded serious, so we threw our packs on our backs and flattened ourselves against the wall. Gran left her supplies scattered in a pile on the ground. A wrangler, who was in the lead, wore a blue cowboy hat. His mule was weighted down with ropes and bright yellow saddlebags.

"Mornin', ma'am." He raised his hand and tipped his hat at Gran.

The mules walked single file with their heads down taking even steps. The people who rode on their backs were all ages, even a couple of kids.

"We're almost to the hitching posts," the wrangler said to the other riders. "We'll stop and let the mules rest there." The mules passed us one at a time. One stepped on a rock. Its hard hoof slid off the edge and the mule lost its footing for a second.

They ambled past us until the fifth in line, with a kid perched on top, looked at Gran and veered wide to avoid

her. The mule slipped, a rock shot under from under its foot, flew through the air, and struck our metal pots on the side of the trail. The clang was ear-splitting.

"Ahhh…" I yelled.

The noises must have scared the deer because it bolted up and ran right off the edge of the trail. The mule had a wild look in its eyes. It must have been as scared as I was. It raced toward the front of the line. Good thing the trail

widened a bit, or the crazed animal would have knocked other mules and riders right over the edge. It bucked past the wrangler, kicking its feet in the air. The kid on its back had his arms wrapped around the mule's neck and his eyes closed. I closed mine too and held my breath.

"OL' BLUE," the wrangler yelled. "Slow down, boy."
The wrangler jumped down, ran past the other riders, gripped
the rope dangling from the mule's bridle, and tugged. "Whoa,
you're okay."

The mule stopped bucking, but the boy didn't let go of
its neck. The wrangler led the mule down to the hitching
posts. The rest of the group followed as if nothing had even
happened.

"Everybody okay?" I asked after the last of the mules had
passed.

"That kid was younger than us," Oz said and looked like
he was about to pass out.

"Well, it's good they have professionals to take care of
situations like that. Let's pass them as soon as possible so
we're out of the way." Gran loaded up the rest of her stuff.

Our pot lid went airborne when the rock hit it. I tried to
help Gran find it, but she shook her head and said it was her
responsibility. I wasn't sure if she if was taking responsibility
for the lost lid or the mule being spooked because our pots
were alongside the trail.

I was glad the mules were tied up when we passed them. We jogged ahead and walked through a red stone arch, the Supai Tunnel. The guidebook said the tunnel was built by the Civilian Conservation Corp in the 1930s. That was the same group who built the wall with the heart-shaped stone at the South Rim.

I looked back through the tunnel to make sure the mules weren't following us. All I saw were cliffs that looked like they were painted with stripes.

"Nate, tell me something to distract me. All I can think about is almost falling to my death when that mule charged me." Oz's hands shook as he filled his water bottle at the Supai fountain.

"Really? The mule charged you? You have quite an imagination," I said.

"Just read us a clue," Oz pleaded.

"We're not supposed to open one until tonight." I tightened the cap on my water bottle. "Gramps assigned these locations because the answers to each riddle correspond to those spots."

"So we don't get the next one until tonight at Cottonwood? But what if I don't make it down the trail. I will die not knowing the answer to the next clue." Oz chugged his water.

"We only know the answer to the first clue. We have no idea which temple, tower, pyramid, or butte. And we still don't know what the night sound is. What makes you think we are going to solve the next one?" Kira asked.

By late morning, we made it to the Redwall Footbridge. It was a high planked bridge with rusted metal railings. Kira gazed into the sky with her binoculars. I didn't see anything except a few puffy clouds and bright blue sky.

After we crossed the bridge, the terrain was different. Dusty paths, sometimes lined with stones along the side, now became steep red drop offs. We walked slowly so that none of us would risk losing our footing. We stopped often to take breaks and so Hope could sit down because she was afraid of heights.

"How can you be afraid of heights? You live in the canyon," Oz asked.

"Yeah, but I don't live up this high. You think I'm this wild canyon girl who scales cliffs, but it's not like that. I'm about as normal as you."

Kira and I looked at each other and laughed. "Oz is the opposite of normal," Kira said.

"Very funny, you guys." Oz tossed a pebble over the edge of the trail and watched it tumble down. "Well, here's your Redwall Limestone. If we were supposed to find it in one particular spot, I think we're in trouble." Oz gestured to the walls that surrounded us on every side.

Redwall Limestone wrapped all the way around the canyon.

Gran stopped in front of a spiny plant growing from the hillside. It was a tall lime-green spike with yellow flowers.

"What's that? It looks like something out of a Dr. Seuss book." I stood next to Gran and fingered the soft flowers on the stalk.

"It does, doesn't it? This is the Kaibab century plant. It grows for eight to ten years, blooms only once, and then it dies."

"It blooms only once in ten years and then the plant dies?"

Gran nodded. "Think about how lucky you are to see it. It usually blooms in May—perfect timing," she said.

"Is it a yucca?" We learned about yuccas in our third-grade American Indian unit.

"My bracelet is made from yucca." Hope's face brightened and she held up her arm.

The Kaibab century plant looked similar to a yucca, but it had sharp spikes on its edges.

"You're close, Nate," Gran said. It's an agave. The indigenous people who lived here dug pits and roasted the plants to eat them."

I eyed the edge of the leaves again. Those spikes didn't look like something I would want to eat. The trail narrowed and we passed between a rock wall and steep hillside where we found a shady spot to stop for lunch.

"My feet feel like they might fall off. How far have we gone?" Kira asked.

"According to the map 4.7 miles, but it feels like a lot farther than that. I always thought going downhill would be the easy part." I pulled off my shoes and rubbed my feet.

"This is where we make a choice," Gran said. "It isn't recommended that day hikers go past this point. Anything farther makes for a long and impossible day hike back out."

"But we're not day hikers," I said. "Let's keep going."

"That's right," Kira, Oz, and Hope said in unison.

After lunch, we followed the trail that ran parallel to the creek. The water wasn't deep enough to be dangerous, and I even filled my fishing hat and dumped it over my head to cool off.

Around a bend, we spotted two buildings and some power lines running along the canyon wall. I didn't think about electricity being in the canyon, but then I read in my trusty guidebook that this power was for the pumping station. The water from Roaring Springs is pumped all the way to the South Rim. Since this was one of our water stops, we filled up our bottles. Gran insisted that we add some electrolyte powder.

"It's hot and we're losing fluids from working so hard." She handed each of us a foil envelope and a handful of pretzels. I poured the purple powder, called Riptide Rush, into my bottle and swished it around. It tasted like grape bubblegum.

"We need to replenish the salts and electrolytes we're losing from sweating. That's the most dangerous part of the hike," she said.

Oz laughed and almost spit his water on Gran. "Sure, that's the most dangerous part. Not almost getting kicked by a crazy mule, or almost getting eaten by a bobcat, or almost falling off the trail that is as narrow as my pack. Electrolyte loss! Sure, that's our problem."

"Just drink your Riptide Rush, Oz. Some of the most dangerous things in nature are the things you can't see," Gran said.

We crossed our last bridge of the day, which spanned the junction of Manzanita Creek and Bright Angel Creek. From here, the trail would be next to Bright Angel Creek all the way to the Colorado River south of Phantom Ranch. For now, we had 1.6 miles left until we reached our home for the night, Cottonwood Campground.

It was only May, but the air felt like a sweltering August night in Chicago. I was relieved when we finally arrived at Cottonwood Campground at 1:30. We were surprised there were no people there. One site did have gear, but no one was around. We picked a site under some trees, which Gran said were cottonwoods. I guess that's where the campground's name came from.

"Let's set up the tents and then we can explore," I said.

"I'm so hot. Can we jump in the creek first? Please, oh great leader!" Oz begged.

"Fine. But then we set up camp." We dropped our packs next to the picnic table and pulled off our shoes and socks. The creek ran right behind our campsite, so it was only a few steps to the water. Even Gran joined in. She waded in with her trekking poles because the wet rocks were slippery. Kira sat down in the water up to her waist.

"This is heaven. I couldn't have walked another step today." She cupped handfuls of water and tossed them onto her head.

"Speaking of steps, we need to decide where we're heading tomorrow," I said.

They looked at each other and groaned. "We just got here. Why are you planning for tomorrow?" Oz asked. "Let's just enjoy this rare moment of nature's air conditioning."

"Speaking of air conditioning, Kira, would you hop out and grab my bandana from my pack?" Gran asked.

Kira pulled herself up from the water and turned to face the campsite. Suddenly she took off sprinting toward the camp, yelling.

"Hey, get away from there. Hey!" Two squirrels perched on top of our packs, both with zippers in their teeth. They weren't the fuzzy squirrels from our North Rim campsite. These looked more like the squirrels we saw in the park at

69

home. We all jumped up and ran. Our sudden movement scared them away.

"This is why I wanted to set up camp."

"Don't be so cranky," Kira said. "Those squirrels didn't take anything."

Why was I the only one who understood the need to follow the rules? I spotted two rusty metal boxes on the picnic table, undid the latches, and pulled off the lids.

"We need to take all the food and anything that smells—like toothpaste or sunscreen—out of our packs and put them in these," I said. "Toiletries in one and food in the other."

Oz tossed in three candy bars and two apples.

"Candy bars? Where did all those come from?" Gran asked.

"I bought them this morning at the store when we were getting the sandwiches for lunch. I gotta have me some sugar. I get hangry without my sweets." Oz shrugged.

"Hangry? What on earth does that mean?" Gran latched the lids of the boxes.

"You know. Hungry and angry. Hangry! Ask Nate, he's seen me when I'm hangry. It's not pretty, Gran," said Oz.

"Hangry or not, this is the first thing we have to do at every campsite. These animals are smart. They know where to find a good meal," I said.

I removed the tent and cook stove from my backpack, which I hung by its strap from an L-shaped pipe that rose from the ground. "Now everyone else, get out what you need to set up the camp and hang your packs over here like this."

"You're getting pretty bossy, Nate," Oz said and gave the girls their tent.

I made Oz sweep the last of the pine needles out of our tent before we explored the camp. The ranger station was empty. According to the guidebook, it's only manned sometimes. We had two nights planned at Cottonwood. This had been Gramps' suggestion. He wanted us to have a long break in case we were hurting after our first day of hiking.

It was getting dark by the time we cooked dinner—macaroni and cheese with rehydrated bell peppers. I looked up at the lights from the North Rim Lodge twinkling miles above us. It made me feel so small to see those tiny pinpricks, and us down in this giant canyon—without a clue about where we were really supposed to be going.

Maybe Gramps' next clue would help. I ripped open the envelope with #4 written on it.

22,25,4,20 / 10,24,21 / 13,17,10,21,8,
10,24,21 / 9,5,11,8,19,21 / 5,22 / 17 / 10,8,25,18,21,9 /
17,8,8,25,12,17,2;
10,24,21,8,21 / 10,5,5 / 17 / 9,10,5,8,21,24,5,11,9,21 /
13,25,10,24 / 8,21,3,4,17,4,10,9 / 5,22 / 9,11,8,12,25,12,17,2.
17,2,2 / 9,6,21,19,25,21,9 / 4,21,21,20 / 17 / 9,25,10,21 /
9,21,19,11,8,21,20 / 22,5,8 / 8,21/2,25,12,17,2.

Oz stared at the paper. "Oh great. Another cipher to decode."

I handed Kira the clue.

"Numbers to letters, it's another cipher. This should be easy. There are three single letter words. I bet they are the word 'a,' so 17 equals A. Nate, where's your notebook?"

I hurried to our tent and came back with it and a pencil.

71

On a new page, I wrote the alphabet with corresponding numbers below the letters starting with 17 and A.

A	B	C	D	E	F	G	H	I	J	K	L	M	N
17	18	19	20	21	22	23	24	25	26	1	2	3	4

O	P	Q	R	S	T	U	V	W	X	Y	Z
5	6	7	8	9	10	11	12	13	14	15	16

Kira and Hope figured out the clue in less than ten minutes.
"How did you do that so fast?" Oz asked.
"We've done it before in math class."
Kira read us the clue.

Find the water, the source of a tribe's arrival;
There too, a storehouse with remnants of survival.
All species need a site secured for revival.

"Can I see that? Besides 'water,' not one word makes sense to me," Oz said.

"Gramps knew we were staying at Cottonwood for two nights, right? Remember, Nate? He's the one who suggested we do that," Kira said. "What kind of water is close to us?"

I pointed at the creek running directly behind us. "Bright Angel Creek is right here."

"No, it can't be that. 'Find the water.' It has to be a different water source," Hope said.

"I was researching day hikes. There are two major sources of water. One is Roaring Springs, which we passed earlier.

There's a spur trail that leads all the way to the spring. Or, Ribbon Falls. It's farther down the trail toward Phantom Ranch."

"Why would Gramps have us head farther down when he knew we were spending two nights here? I vote for Roaring Springs," Oz said.

"But why would he have us backtrack?" Kira asked.

I shook my head. "I think we need to think about it. We're only talking about the first line of the clue. There are lots of other instructions here. I vote we sleep on it and decide tomorrow."

We cleaned up our scraps from dinner and secured our storage box lids. In the tent, I listened to Oz narrate his reality show in an Australian accent. I didn't tell him to be quiet because I knew I wouldn't be sleeping much. I kept turning on the flashlight and reading the clue.

The girls and Gran finally turned off their lights, and Oz snored quietly next to me.

I had almost nodded off when I heard a yelp. It sounded like it was coming from Gran's tent. The yelp turned to a shriek, and when I poked my head outside the door of our tent, Gran's tent was lurching around next to ours. She was like a worm trapped inside a giant cocoon, but the cocoon's door unzipped and things started flying out.

"Get it off of me!" Gran yelled.

GRAVEL DUG INTO MY BARE FEET when I jumped out of the tent. By the time I reached her, Gran was squatting in the front of her tent with her flashlight pointed at the back corner. Hope knelt beside her with a hand on Gran's back.

"It's okay. I'll get it," Hope said in her usual soft voice.

A lizard as long as my forearm crouched on Gran's sleeping bag. It had bright green scales with bands of red and black around its neck. Red dots covered its body like someone had dripped paint on it.

"I was dreaming that spiders were crawling all over me, and then I woke up and saw that thing. I couldn't catch it. It was running around on its back feet like a person inside the tent."

"She could feel the heat from your body. She's just trying to stay warm," Hope inched toward the lizard, who sat as still as a statue in the beam of Gran's light.

"How do you know it's a she?" I asked.

"See those red splotches on her body? It's a collared lizard, and the females get those spots when they are carrying eggs," Hope whispered.

Kira's head appeared behind me. "She's pregnant? That's awesome."

Gran took a deep breath. "Awesome, but not in my sleeping bag. How's it going, Hope?"

Hope eased alongside the lizard but left a clear path to the door of the tent.

"Keep shining your light. I think she'll make a run for it." Hope clapped her hands. The lizard cocked its head to one side and rose on her hind legs. She ran on her back feet, her front ones dangling loosely, and a tail as long as her body flew through the air behind her. She looked like Kermit the Frog in a fifty-yard dash.

After the eventful night with the lizard, which Oz slept right through, things were slow going the next morning. When I crawled out of my tent, Hope was sitting at the table writing.

"Another letter to your grandmother? Did you tell her about the lizard?" I asked.

"Yes, and other things on our trip. I spend the school year so far away from my family, it helps them to hear about all the things I'm doing."

"Isn't it weird being here… so close to where you live… and not being with them?"

"It's strange. Like last night with the lizard. I've never seen one of those without someone from my family being there. I'm excited to go home for the summer when our hike is over." She slid her letter closer so that I could read what it said.

Words crawled across the page just like in my notebook,

but Hope's writing was loopy and curling. Her letter was divided by days, and it described the deer from the day before and the squirrels on our packs.

"I never expected to see so much wildlife. I always think of Grand Canyon as a desert. Who knew there were so many animals here?" I asked.

"I did," said Hope quietly. "That's what's hard about living in California. Sure I miss my parents and my brother, but I grew up surrounded by these animals. They're like my friends. A squirrel lives near our house in Supai, and it comes every day to beg for food." Her face flushed and I could see she was on the verge of tears.

I wasn't sure how to make her feel better. After all, I couldn't imagine having to leave everything I knew behind just to go to school. "This stuff about the deer and the squirrels would be great to include in the legend. Maybe you should write the next part."

I pushed my notebook to her so she could read what I'd written so far. I hoped to take her mind off how sad she was. She turned the pages slowly and looked at me wide-eyed.

"Nate, what's up with these lists?" She flipped through the pages near the front of the book. "Do they all connect?"

"That's exactly what I'm trying to figure out. These are all the clues so far:

Redwall limestone; one of these temples; something in the soundscape. And now, we have to figure out what this water source is that we're looking for."

"I was thinking about that last night. Roaring Springs and Ribbon Falls are both waterfalls, but only one has a 'storehouse with remnants of survival' and is a 'source of a tribe's arrival,'" Hope said.

"What do you mean?" I asked.

"My uncle taught me that most tribes have an origin story. The Havasupai believe that our people originated from a spring near the San Francisco Peaks, north of Flagstaff."

"What does that have to do with this clue?" I asked.

"Well, if you think about it, 'place of origin' and 'source of tribe's arrival' are basically the same thing."

I thought about what Hope said. "True."

"Many years ago, the ancestors of the Havasupai and the Zuni Tribes lived in harmony. The Zuni believed that their place of origin was at Ribbon Falls."

I sat in silence, stunned. Hope was beginning to make sense. She stood up from the picnic table, and paced in a circle, rubbing her bracelet while she talked.

"There are granaries around Ribbon Falls—places where the native people stored food," she said.

All the pieces seemed to fit. American Indian granaries could definitely be 'storehouses with remnants for survival.'

"You're a genius!" I grabbed Hope and hugged her. She stood stiff like a board, but then patted me twice on the back before she walked away. By that time, Kira and Oz were awake and Gran had returned from her morning walk.

"Hope figured it out. We are definitely heading to Ribbon Falls today." I consulted the map while Hope explained her logic to the rest of the group.

As I ate breakfast, I made a list of all the things I could find in my book about Ribbon Falls: travertine dome, moss, waterfall, granary, water birds. I was anxious to get up there and start looking for something that might explain what 'All species need a site secured for revival' meant.

"We only need daypacks today because we'll be back here long before dinner. Everybody make yourself a sandwich and be sure to fill up your water bottles," I said.

I loaded an apple, some jerky, and a few granola bars into my pack. When I headed toward the water pump to refill my bottles, Oz was standing barefoot in the creek. He held a sock in his hand that looked like it had a heavy weight in the bottom. His water bottle was balanced on a rock near the creek bank, and Oz was wringing drops of water from his sock into the bottle.

"What are you doing?"

Oz looked casually at me and continued wringing out his sock.

"You told me to fill up with water. I couldn't find our water pump to filter the creek water, so I thought I would try this Wildman trick. He fills up his sock with sand, and the sand acts as a natural filter when he wrings the water out of the bottom."

"That is almost as disgusting as drinking your own pee. We don't need to filter. There's a water spigot so that you don't have to drink stinky sock water."

I filled my own bottles with fresh water from the spigot. Oz was still wringing his sock when I went back to store the breakfast supplies. I put the lids back on the storage boxes and was latching them when I heard Kira say, "Are you drinking water from your sock?"

I looked back at Oz dripping water from the bottom of his sock straight into his mouth.

"What? These are clean socks," he said.

According to my watch it was 9 a.m. I could already feel the heat reflecting off the canyon walls. Back on the North Kaibab Trail, which wound back and forth around the sloping walls above us, we dodged cactus blooming with yellow and pink flowers.

After about half a mile, we dropped down to a boulder-filled area where the creek ran smooth and steady. We crawled from boulder to boulder to cross, and soon the trail opened up to a wide flat section with big rock formations in the distance. After forty-five minutes, we arrived at a sign for Ribbon Falls, a wooden bridge straight ahead, and the creek far below it. A black bird swooped above us. It circled and then flew off.

Kira, of course, had her binoculars out.

"What's the word, Miss Ornithologist? Condor or wobbly bird?" Oz asked.

Kira smiled, but looked disappointed. "Just a turkey vulture." I checked the compass on my watch. We were hiking northwest, and the bird disappeared to the southwest.

Ten more minutes of tramping through bushy trees, and we saw the waterfall. It almost looked like two waterfalls. The highest one fell from a jagged red rock wall above. Underneath was the dome that my book described. The travertine rock, covered in fluorescent green moss, rose like a huge dome that must have been 100 feet high. The water flowed into a pool at the bottom of the falls.

We dropped our packs and waded into the cold water.

"Dude, look at this." Oz crouched at the foot of the dome where the moss parted like a green curtain, and he disappeared inside.

"Where'd you go?"

Oz's stuck his hand out from under the moss. I followed him into a passage piled high with rocks. We tried to climb toward the sunlight above, but it was too slippery to get a grip. A tiny gray bird dove under the water.

"I didn't know birds could swim," Oz said.

"What about ducks?" I asked.

"That's different. Ducks aren't really birds, are they?"

Oz followed the bird out into the open until it disappeared under the shallow water where it hunted for insects.

"It's called an American dipper. Gramps loved them," Gran called out from where she sat at the side of the pool. I waded over to the edge and climbed out to sit next to her.

Under the shade of the large cliff overhang from where the water fell, Gran munched on a banana.

"Hungry?" she asked.

I took a bite and handed it back to her.

"Finish it. I have another one." She stared down into the pool where Oz swam below. "Everything looks so different," she said.

"What do you mean?"

"It's the first time I've been to any of these places without Gramps. His eyes were always glued to the sky—just like Kira. So I'm seeing everything in a whole new way without him." She reached up to touch the necklace that hung from her neck.

I swallowed hard and wiped my eyes with the back of my hand. I had kept myself so busy thinking about Gramps' clues, so I didn't have to think about missing him.

"Tell me about your neck-lace." The gold chain around her neck had a charm with two owls sitting side by side on a branch. "I've never seen you wear it at home."

"I pulled it out for this trip. Gramps gave it to me just before he died, along with that letter for you kids." She pulled the charm back and forth along the chain. "I thought it would be like bring-ing a piece of him here with me."

Gran stood up and called to the rest of the group. "What have you discovered about the clue?"

We met Kira, Hope, and Oz down by our packs.

"What are we looking for, anyway?" Oz whined.

"We don't know exactly, but we know this is the right waterfall because there are granaries around here some-where," I said.

"Yes, but what are we supposed to find?" Kira was pacing in circles.

"The clue doesn't say, but I haven't seen anything so far that seems to fit. Maybe it's farther from the falls. I say we head back toward the bridge," I said.

We found a footpath and followed it for a mile. The creek was clear and filled with tadpoles and small fish. The clouds moved in, blocking the sun from view, and the sky changed from overcast to black. A low rumble sounded in the distance. The wind blew hard now and the water in the creek changed from clear to a muddy brown color.

Suddenly the hair on the back of my neck stood up. My nose filled with the smell of rusty metal. A bright flash lit up the sky. It was followed by a crash that echoed throughout the canyon. The air was charged with electricity. Rain started to fall, and then another crash of thunder. We needed to find shelter fast.

Oz and I ran up the trail toward a rock wall in front of us. The girls and Gran followed. Raindrops pelted us, and I searched for a protected area. Another bolt of lightning lit up the sky, this time at the base of a tree in front of us.

"Over here," yelled Gran. She looked terrified as she sprinted away from the path. She climbed up the rocks and huddled on a ledge about five feet off the ground. The rain came down in sheets. Drops so close together, I could barely see my hand in front of me. There was no break between thunder claps so it sounded like the canyon was filled with bass drums.

Gran put her arms around us and pulled us closer to her. A rock overhang guarded us from the rain, but the water sliding off of the face created a waterfall that blocked our view.

Oz whimpered whenever the thunder crashed.

"What does Wildman say about lightning?" I asked and tried to take his attention off of the raging storm.

"Wildman says seek cover or get inside." Oz rocked back and forth.

Behind him there were small openings in the rocks. When I looked more closely I could see that they were man-made rocks, like bricks piled on top of each other.

"Look. We can get inside," said Oz. Another flash of lightning and Oz knelt down and started to crawl.

"No," we all yelled.

"These must be the granaries we read about. You can't go in there, Oz. It's a protected site," I said.

Instead we crowded under the overhang near the granaries and watched the rain turn the path in front of us into a river. For twenty minutes, I tried to step out from under the overhang, but each time I set a toe into the sheets of rain, another bolt of lightning came down right in front of us. The girls screamed and Oz sat with his hand over his ears. We were trapped.

THE SKY LIT UP WITH LIGHTNING, and I counted the seconds until I heard the crack of thunder. For a long time, the thunder was constant, but after an hour, I could count three seconds in between.

"Why are you counting?" Hope asked.

"To see if the storm is moving farther away." I checked my watch.

"Okay, but why count?" Oz said.

"It's called the flash-to-bang method. I learned about it on the Weather Channel. Light travels at more than 180,000 miles per second, but sound only travels at little more than 1,000 feet per second. You wait for the flash of lightning. Count the number of seconds until you hear the thunder, and divide that by five. The answer should tell you how many miles from here the storm is," I said. "Try it."

At the next flash of lightning, we all counted: 1-Mississippi, 2-Mississippi, 3-Mississippi. The sound of thunder echoed in the distance.

"Three seconds divided by five means the storm is more than half a mile from here," Kira said. "That's great news."

"Yeah, but it feels like an eternity since we ate, and I'm starving. Do we have anything to eat?" Oz dug through his backpack. We had eaten all of our lunch and snacks earlier. I found a granola bar smashed at the bottom of my pack.

"Here. This is all I have left."

"Why didn't you tell us to bring more food, Mr. Group Leader."

"Gimme a break, I didn't know we'd be stranded here." I tore open the wrapper and divided the bar into five pieces. They were little, but I hoped that along with Gran's apple, we would be able to last until we got back to camp.

Thirty minutes later the storm was two miles away. Unfortunately, the sky wasn't any lighter and the rain continued to fall.

"We've been sitting here for hours. I think we should try to head back to camp," I said.

"If we can get back to camp..." Oz whined.

"Oh no, we're not spending the night here. I'm already freezing, and imagine how much colder it's going to get later," Kira said.

"Calm down, Kira. We will do what we have to do to stay safe. It may not be smart to go anywhere right now." Gran tightened her arm around Kira's shoulder.

"I think we should vote. If we don't see any lightning in the next twenty minutes, we head down. Show of hands."

Kira and Oz raised their hands. Hope and Gran just stared at me. I raised my hand to break the tie.

"Okay, it's decided." I set the timer on my watch for twenty minutes and chewed my granola bar slowly. I wished I hadn't eaten so much of my lunch.

Oz paced back and forth peering into the openings of the granary.

"Oz, what are you doing?" asked Hope.

"Looking for anything left in this granary. I would be happy to chew on some old corn kernels." He sounded desperate as he put his head in the dark opening between the stacked bricks and shined the light from his cell phone into the darkness. "If I could just see in there, I might find something."

"Ah..." Oz screamed and jumped backwards as a black cloud flew out of the granary. He hopped from foot to foot and rubbed his hands in his red hair. "What are those?"

Before any of us could help him, the cloud of animals was gone. Kira made her way along the ledge and peered into the opening.

"Those were bats, Oz." Kira said.

"Bats? What if one had bitten me? I'd turn into a vampire."

Kira shook her head. "But they didn't. Besides, they weren't that kind of bats."

"How can you be so calm? I could be morphing into Dracula."

"I rely on my understanding of proven scientific theories. And science has definitely proven that you can't turn into a vampire."

"That doesn't make me feel any better," Oz said.

"Give me a light." Kira held out her hand. "I can't see a thing."

I passed her my flashlight.

"Thanks. You're always prepared," she said.

That made me feel a little better about not being prepared for the dinner hour at Ribbon Falls.

"Look, there are eggshells in here. Talk about 'place of origin.' Looks like something originated right here in this granary."

I moved closer to Kira. The flashlight lit up a pile of crushed brown eggshells. I wondered what type of bird they were from. Gramps would know. But suddenly I knew something even more important.

"A nest. Gramps wanted us to come to Ribbon Falls, the place of origin, to find a storehouse with remnants of survival where there was a site secured for revival," I said.

"Bats and broken eggshells are secured for revival? This isn't making any sense," Oz said.

"We know that Gramps studied birds, right? What is a bird's place of origin?"

"An egg?" Kira said. Her face looked like she had found the right spot for a puzzle piece.

"Yes, and those eggs are found where?"

"In a 'place secured for revival' or birth. A nest," Hope said. "I think he wanted us to look for a nest."

"But this nest? He must have known that birds always roost here. We just need to figure out what kind of bird these eggs belong to and find a second nest somewhere else."

"If we are looking for a nest for this bird, it's not a condor," Kira said. "They lay blueish-white eggs and besides they nest high above the ground. I also don't think this is remote enough for them."

"Speaking of your beloved condors, I think we saw the true nature of the thunderbird tonight," Oz said.

"What are you talking about?" Kira asked.

"Remember you said that the thunderbirds create thunder and lightning with a flap of their wings. Maybe that wasn't a turkey vulture we saw earlier. Maybe it was a condor telling us to quit following it. This storm is a pretty clear message to me. *Whoooo*," Oz held his hands up and made a noise like a ghost.

"Whatever. I don't think the nest Gramps wants us to find is here because we still have four clues left to figure out." I looked at my watch. "And it's time to go."

We inched across the slippery rock ledge and back to the path, but it wasn't a path anymore. Water streamed past us. On the now submerged rocks we climbed up earlier, it was slow going. To make it down the steeper part, we all sat on our butts like a baby goes down stairs. In the distance, water poured over the edge of Ribbon Falls and the sound was deafening.

Just as quickly as the storm had come, the skies cleared up. Thankfully a full moon appeared and helped light the way. We couldn't use our flashlights all the time because we needed our hands to grab hold of scrub brush. By the time we reached the bridge, it was dark and we were soaked, freezing in fact. The air was cold and the wind hadn't stopped blowing yet.

From the main trail, it had taken us forty-five minutes in the morning to hike to the bridge; now we had to leap back and forth over the waters on the flat part. We fell into a silent rhythm. All I wanted was to climb into my warm sleeping bag back at our campsite.

"It's quiet back there. Everybody doing okay?" I called over my shoulder.

"Just freezing and ready to eat something," Hope said.

"So, when Wildman falls in the river, he always strips down and builds a fire."

"We're not doing either of those things, Oz. We don't need to be running naked through the campsite, plus you know we can't have fires in the canyon. We do need to get warm quickly when we get back, so put on dry clothes. I'll boil some water so we can eat something warm. You never know what the weather's going to be like in the canyon. We should have packed rain gear and extra clothes. None of us were thinking as well as we should have," Gran said.

She was talking to the group, but it felt like she was talking to me. Some leader I was. You're always so prepared, Nate. I was too excited when we left camp. If I hadn't been in such a hurry, we wouldn't be trudging along this trail like hungry wet rats.

The sign for Cottonwood Campground finally came into view. The trail was a lot drier so we made a break for it.

I headed straight for the tent to put on dry clothes but stopped before I made it there. Strewn on the ground were candy bar wrappers—Oz's candy bar wrappers. Something glinted on the picnic bench. I raised my flashlight and stared at four pairs of yellow eyes. They belonged to a group of animals that looked like a combination of a raccoon and a cat. One large one and three babies stood on top of our tipped-over storage box munching our food.

"Pesky ring-tailed cat," Hope said and ran toward them.

Gran and Kira clapped their hands and yelled. The thieves raced off.

"I've never seen anything like that." Kira bent down and picked up apple cores and bits of foil under the picnic table.

"Unfortunately, there are probably more of them around here. Just like the squirrels, they're always looking for food," Hope said.

The campground was a mess. At least we had zipped our tents, but *I* was the last one to put things in the food box before we left in the morning. Oz was dripping sock water into his mouth, and I must have left the lid unlatched when I got distracted. I knelt to see more closely what was left of our food.

One piece of jerky was on top of a torn-open Ziploc. Our foil packets were empty with their contents scattered on the ground.

"Hey, those things ate all my candy bars," Oz said.

I pounded my hand on the table. "Your candy bars and your stupid sock water are the reason they ate our food."

Oz's face turned red. "This isn't my fault. You're the one who didn't close the box, Nate."

"It's not my fault either." But I realized that maybe all of it was my fault: the food, the soaking wet clothes. I threw the box onto the ground.

"Nate, calm down," Gran said.

"Why? You said it yourself. We should have been more prepared. I'm the leader. You said that too. What kind of a leader doesn't secure the food, or pack extra supplies for a day hike? And I was the tie-breaking vote. I'm the one who said we needed to leave the falls. It's my fault we ended up soaked. Some leader I turned out to be."

"I DON'T KNOW WHY they didn't eat the rice?" Oz tossed a few grains into his mouth, and sucked on them. "It's not any worse than when we ate the dehydrated food without water, Nate." He patted me on the back.

He was trying to make laugh when all I wanted to do was cry.

"So, Oz what would Wildman do in a situation like this?" Kira asked.

Oz knitted his eyebrows. "He'd say 'No big deal, mate. If we need food, we'll find it.' Then he'd go bite the head off a scorpion or something."

We cleaned up the mess, but more ringtails waited in the shadows, probably hoping we'd share what we had left with them.

Gran's head lamp lit up the remaining food lined up on the picnic table: two jars of peanut butter, all of our electro-lyte powder (I guess Riptide Rush isn't popular with ringtails), rice, and mac-and-cheese (those were stored in a plastic con-tainer that the animals couldn't figure out how to open). We had no bread, and no fruit and only three granola bars.

"It's not enough. We should turn back to the North Rim to restock at the store or just call off the trip altogether," I said. It had been a fun adventure when it was just about clues and exploring, but now it was about our survival and I wasn't sure I wanted to be the group leader anymore.

"Were you not listening to me, mate?" Oz sifted through the storage box where we'd put our toiletries. "Look, here's a whole bag of energy bars. We must have tossed those in here accidentally." He tore open the package and bit into one. "Tastes a little like sunscreen from being cooked in this box all day, but it'll do."

"Nate, you know I'm responsible for your safety, but I think we can make this work. We have enough for three dinners. We can buy food at the canteen in Phantom Ranch for our lunches and two nights there. If we ration this out, we'll be eating a lot of peanut butter and rice, but we won't starve," Gran said.

"Yeah, dude. Wildman always says, 'It's about improvising. Things rarely go according to plan.' So we'll make a new plan. I vote that we vote." He swiped my hat and headed for the creek.

"All in favor of turning back?" Kira said. I shot my hand up as quickly as I could. If it came down to a tie, I didn't want to be the tie-breaking vote again. No one else raised their hand, though.

"Captain, you're outvoted. Will you retake the helm and give us our marching orders?" Oz tossed my hat in my direction and saluted.

I wasn't happy about it, but I couldn't fight the rest of the group.

In the morning, I showed everyone our route on the map. We headed south. For the first part of the hike, we retraced our steps from the night before. The sun was shining and there wasn't even any standing water. That's the desert for you, I guess.

"I can't believe this is the same place we were last night," Kira said. She wiped the sweat from her eyes and chugged her water. "Someone needs to have a talk with Mother Nature and tell her to make up her mind."

"No, someone needs to tell your precious thunderbirds to quit messing with the weather. Hot is fine with me, but flash floods are not my idea of a good time. Next thing you know it will be snowing. Condors don't create snow too, do they?" Oz asked.

"I don't think you have to worry about that, Oz. It doesn't snow here," I said.

"It snows on the rims in the winter, and it even snows in Supai." Hope tied her hair into a pile on the top of her head.

"No way? It snows in Supai…down in the canyon?" I asked.

"Sure, but only once or twice a year. We all stand in the middle of the basketball court at school and catch snowflakes in our mouths. We don't get to do it very often. That's why I can't believe you don't get excited about snow in Chicago."

Ahead of us was a section of the trail where snow would be welcomed by all of us—The Box. My guidebook said this area heats up to temperatures above 100 degrees. We had decided to wait until The Box to open the next clue. I hoped it would distract us from how hot we were.

"Make sure you're drinking. The ringtails ate our salty snacks—the pretzels—so please eat a couple of spoonfuls of peanut butter instead," Gran said.

"We know," we all said together.

The canyon walls rose up around us and the heat felt like we were cooking from the inside out. The rocks were scorching—I could have cooked an egg on them if that ringtail hadn't cracked them all. We found a shady overhang to stop, and I pulled out the next clue.

Eight times across a bridge with the Cherub Creek below,
Before you reach the river, decide which way to go.
You're searching for a trail to the east or to the west,
which leads you to a waterway, please try to pick the best.

"Eight times across a bridge with the Cherub Creek below? 'Cherub?' That must be Bright Angel Creek, right? So how many bridges have we crossed?" I grabbed my map—happy to be back in the hunt for answers.

We counted: Redwall Footbridge, the bridge after Roaring Springs, the bridge at Ribbon Falls.

"Are you sure the bridge to Ribbon Falls crossed Bright Angel Creek?" Kira asked.

I ran my finger down the map, "Yes."

"But we crossed it twice. Once in the morning and once last night," Hope said. "How many times do we count it?"

I shivered at the thought of our damp nighttime crossing. My finger traced the Bright Angel Trail from Cottonwood Campground to Phantom Ranch.

"We cross four more footbridges before we reach Phantom Ranch today. So that's seven," I said.

"Or eight. If you count twice across at Ribbon Falls," Hope said.

"But then we have to cross the suspension bridge to get across the Colorado River, so that would be eight." Kira said.

"No, Kira. The clue says, 'before you reach the river decide which way to go.' So the trail that we're looking for has to be *before* the river."

"Are you sure?" Kira leaned toward me and pushed my fingers out of the way. She studied the map. "According to the clue, we're to search for a trail to the east or to the west that leads to a waterway. There is only one trail before the Colorado River that leads to a waterway." She pointed to a long trail, which wound off to the east toward Clear Creek.

"So that has to be it. 'Before you reach the river decide which way to go.' Plus, look at the end of the trail: Zoroaster Temple. The trail practically ends at a temple and a waterway." I was so excited that we'd solved the clue.

"Wait a minute," Kira pushed my finger down the map to the trails south of the Colorado River, "there are two choices leading to water down here. This trail leads west and this one leads east. Gramps wouldn't have said east *or* west if there wasn't a choice. I think we *decide* before we cross the river and then we take action after we cross the suspension bridge—the *eighth time* across." I pulled the map from Kira and folded it up. There was no convincing her of things once she had her mind made up. I would just have to find another way to prove that the Clear Creek Trail was correct. I stood up to start hiking again. The rest of the group followed.

"Sure, Nate. Put the map away when you don't get your way. What do you guys think?" Kira asked. Oz and Hope looked at each other and stared back at us.

"No more fighting about it. Nate's the map guy. Maybe he's right," Oz said.

I could tell that Kira didn't like that answer, so she looked for a better one. "Gran, what do you think?"

"I think the two of you had better come to an agreement, but we have more important things to think about right now. I think there's a snake on the trail up there."

I stopped and Gran squeezed past me.

"Don't move. That's more than just a snake. It looks like a rattler." Gran motioned toward a spiky bush on the side of the trail. "Maybe he's out looking for his lunch."

"Oh, please don't talk about lunch. If I have to eat any more peanut butter, I'm going to barf," Oz said.

We all shushed him. The snake was a pale shade of pink and had outlines of brown ovals running the length of its body. I wasn't even sure it was a rattlesnake, until it coiled its head back and we heard a noise like a baby's rattle.

"He's not happy that we're here," Hope said and backed away. She paced in a circle.

"Everybody just stay calm and maybe he'll leave."

"I would prefer if we leave," Kira said. "Coiling means he feels threatened."

"Of course he does. I'd feel threatened too if I thought giants were keeping me from finding my lunch," said Oz.

We all stayed frozen, and the snake stayed coiled for a few minutes but didn't seem to be able to resist going off in

another direction to look for food. It slithered into the bush, and I ran back to get Hope. She still paced and mumbled to herself. We plastered ourselves against the wall opposite where the snake had been and made our way safely past.

After the snake, we crossed four footbridges. Even though the trail was pretty flat, my pack felt even heavier than it had on the first day. Since there was no available water between Cottonwood and Phantom Ranch, we had loaded up our bottles before we left the campsite. We also didn't want to take the chance that our water filter might clog if we relied on pumping water from the Bright Angel Creek.

My watch read 1:35 p.m. when we reached a small wooden sign for Clear Creek Trail. It also said no camping on the trail for 2 miles. We had half a mile left on the North Kaibab Trail until we reached Phantom Ranch.

"Can we stop here?" I asked. "I'd like to look at the beginning of the Clear Creek Trail. We might see something that would help us figure out if this is where Gramps wanted us to go." I thought if I asked rather than insisted, I might get some agreement. The group slowed to a stop.

"Can't this wait? We only have half a mile left. We can come back here later… after I eat something and suck down ten glasses of water." Oz doused his baseball hat with water from one of his bottles and tugged it back onto his head.

"Please. Just give me fifteen minutes." I was tired too, but this was the last trail before the river. I felt like Gramps was leading us here. "Oz, I'll buy you ice cream when we get to Phantom Ranch."

Oz's face brightened. "I'm in. Anything for ice cream."

"Girls, do you want to wait here and look for rattlesnakes, or are you coming with us?" I knew this would convince Hope to keep walking. She pushed past me toward the sign.

"Let's go," she said.

"Gran and Kira. That leaves you two."

"We'll go with you, Nate, but I'll only give you ten minutes. It's hot and we need to be finished hiking for the day." I was grateful and relieved that Gran had agreed. I just knew we'd find something.

The trail climbed steeply and within five minutes I wondered if this was such a good idea. We slogged around the first switchback and saw a man lying on his side on a steep slope just off the edge of the trail. He wore a tank top, running shorts, and an orange baseball hat. A water tube dangled from a small backpack that sat on the trail above him.

"Hey," I yelled down the side of the trail. "Are you okay?" The man groaned but he didn't respond. We dropped our packs and hurried to the edge of the trail.

"Sir. Sir," Gran called. "Are you hurt?"

The man groaned again, lifted his head and looked at us.

"Sir. Are you alright?" Gran asked. "Can you make it up here?" The man pushed himself onto his knees and crawled toward the trail. His face was scratched and bleeding from the cactus he had fallen on.

"I... I... can't." He collapsed on the slope just a foot below us. I scooted off the trail and dug my feet into the loose gravel. I could easily creep down to where his head was. His eyes were open. His breathing was fast but uneven.

"Hey, can you hear me?" I asked. The man nodded, but when he tried to speak, no words came out.

"Take this. It might be heat exhaustion." Gran slid down the slope to where I sat and handed me her water bottle.

"It's okay. We'll help you." Gran edged the man onto his back and put her arm under his head as he sipped from the bottle. Oz took off his shirt and poured water onto it. He wrapped the shirt around the man's head to shade him from the sun.

"Gran," Kira dropped her pack and knelt down next to us, "should we get help?"

"Hang on, Kira. This water might make a difference."

Within a few minutes, the blank stare in the man's eyes disappeared.

"Can you sit up?" I asked.

"I think so."

We grabbed his arms and helped him through the cactus to the trail.

"What were you doing out here?" Gran asked him.

"We are running rim-to-rim today."

"Where is the rest of your group?"

"They took a break at Phantom Ranch. I told them I would continue on," he said in a weak voice.

I handed him the water bottle and he took another drink.

"But you're not even on the right trail," Oz said.

"I must have taken a wrong turn. I just need to get back to my friends. I'll be fine."

He reached forward to push himself up from the ground. Oz and I jumped up and each took one of his arms to steady him. When he got upright his pale face dripped with sweat. He teetered for a second and then lurched forward. We tightened our grip and the girls tried to help, but he crumpled to the ground.

C H A P T E R

12

THE MAN'S EYELIDS FLUTTERED.
He was breathing but not responding to our yells.

"You know I don't believe in splitting up, but we have to get help. Oz and Nate, you will stay with me. Kira and Hope, empty my pack. Leave three water bottles with us. Load up the rest and fill them. Find a ranger and tell them exactly where we are." Gran's voice was serious.

The girls followed her instructions and ran down the trail.

"Be careful and stay together," Gran yelled at their backs.

"Boys, help me get him rolled onto his side." We eased the man to the ground.

Oz dumped his pack and parts from our tent all over the trail.

"He needs shade. That's the first thing Wildman talks about is finding shade when you are suffering from heat exhaustion." Oz held the rain fly from our tent in the air. A blue shadow from the fabric fell on the man's head and face.

"It's not great but it's better than nothing. Good thinking, Oz." Gran said. She picked up Oz's wet shirt that was now on the ground. "Put this back on. I don't want you getting sunburned."

I held the rain fly while Oz did as Gran asked.

My water bottle was still half full, so Gran poured it on the man's face. He sputtered and opened his eyes. He looked dazed, but at least he wasn't unconscious.

"Get the map and use it to fan his face, Nate. We need to get his body temperature cooled down as much as possible. Oz, take over the rain fly," Gran said.

We were in the middle of the trail, so when the man finally sat up, Gran and I helped him to a big rock near the side of the trail.

"What happened?" He focused his eyes on my face.

"I think you passed out. You scared us." Now that the guy was talking I could feel my hands start to shake. I gripped the map tighter, fanned faster, and hoped it would calm my nerves.

Oz paced and waved his cell phone in the air. He was trying to get a signal to call 9-1-1.

"Nothing. This thing doesn't do us any good."

"I'm glad you tried, Oz. You never know where a signal might pop up. Let's just hope the girls made it to Phantom Ranch safely," Gran said.

"You should go find them," the man said. "I'll be fine."

"You are not remotely fine, and we're not going anywhere. In fact, if you start to feel light-headed, put your head between your knees." I could tell Gran was nervous. That's when she gets bossy. And when Gran is bossy, people listen.

After two full hats of water poured on his head and a lot of electrolyte powder in his hydration pouch, the guy seemed to have a little life back. We took turns holding the rainfly over Brian—that was his name—and fanning him with the map. I looked at my watch every minute, wishing that we had some way to communicate with the girls. I begged Gran to let me look for them, but she insisted that we didn't need to be split up even more.

"The girls will be fine. They are level-headed and strong hikers," she said, nodding to make herself feel better.

And she was right. After twenty more glances at my watch, I heard voices.

Hope and Kira led the pack. My knees went weak because I was so relieved to see them. Behind them were two rangers who each carried bags of supplies and a group of three men, all dressed in shorts and tank tops like Brian.

The next few minutes were a blur of activity. The rangers put a needle in Brian's arm and held a bag of clear liquid over his head. For hydration, the ranger explained. They wrapped his arms in cold packs like the ones the nurse uses when you hurt yourself at school. Gran filled them in on exactly what had happened after the girls left. Brian's friends crowded around and took over holding the rainfly for shade.

"You are lucky these kids," the ranger looked at Gran, "and woman found you and were such quick thinkers. All the things they did to get you cooled off and hydrated might have saved your life. Heat exhaustion can quickly turn to heat stroke, and that can be deadly."

Once we knew Brian was safely in good hands, there wasn't much left for us to do. Gran and I hugged the girls, and Oz put his arms around their shoulders. We repacked our bags and headed down the trail for Phantom Ranch.

"You guys were fast. Did you sprint the whole way?" I

asked.

"Hope was like a track star," Kira said. "I've never seen you move that quickly. I was just trying to keep up."

"I was scared. I knew if we didn't get help fast for that man, he could be in big trouble."

"We saw those other guys dressed like him and figured they must be his friends. They helped us find the ranger," Kira said.

"You were all very brave. I'm just glad we were there. I hate to think what would have happened to Brian if we hadn't found him," Gran said.

I don't know if Gramps was trying to tell us something or if Clear Creek Trail was the answer to the riddle, but I'm sure glad we detoured up there.

The half mile to Phantom Ranch went fast. We traded stories with Kira and Hope about what happened on their rescue run and what we did to help Brian. A stone trail lined with prickly pear cactus greeted us along with the 'Welcome to Phantom Ranch' sign. I've never been happier to see signs of civilization. Feeling helpless out on the trail made me realize just how self-reliant you need to be in the backcountry.

The girls told Oz about the Phantom Ranch Canteen. He quickly forgot our rescue scare.

"You promised me ice cream, Nate. And that's the first thing we're going to do."

The Phantom Ranch Canteen is an old cabin. The thermometer outside read 95 degrees, and I could only imagine how hot it was when we were on the trail. We dropped our packs and bought big cups of lemonade, but there was no ice cream for Oz. The lemonade was sweet and sour and so cold in my mouth it gave me a brain freeze. In all the years that Oz and I had lemonade stands in our neighborhood, I don't think I ever tasted a better drink than the one at Phantom Ranch. We also bought sandwiches and scarfed them down in record time.

Phantom Ranch is like Grand Central Station—but filled with hikers (like us), mule riders arriving from the South Rim, and rafters coming off the Colorado River. Everyone seemed excited to hear about the adventures of others.

We hiked another half mile through Phantom Ranch to our campsite at Bright Angel Campground along the creek. We remembered the curious squirrels at Cottonwood and decided to suffer through the heat to set up camp before we got to the business of cooling off in the creek.

After our tents were ready, the rest of our food stored, and I had checked the storage can lid five times, we were dripping with sweat. We sat in the cold water. Kira screamed, of course, but she wasn't the only one. Squeals echoed up and down Bright Angel Creek as people cooled off. My feet were frozen, but it was like a medicine that numbed my bruised toes and the blisters from so much walking.

We couldn't stay away from the Canteen and that lemonade. On our second trip, we turned in our Junior Ranger booklets. Mom and Dad had taken me to lots of national parks, but this was the best Junior Ranger patch I'd earned. I didn't know any other kids who've hiked to the bottom of Grand Canyon. This patch would have a special place on my expedition shelf back home.

A leather satchel hung near the counter with a sign above it: 'Phantom Ranch. Mailed by mule. Outgoing mail goes here.'

"I was reading about this. It's the only place in the US where mail is delivered by mule."

"That's not exactly true," Hope said quietly. "Supai has the only *real* mule-driven mail service. We can get packages, food, things from online. Mail call is once a day when the pack mules arrive in town."

"What if I wanted ice cream sandwiches delivered. How would they keep those cold?"

"Two ways. The big loads are for the Canteen. They store the food in a deep freezer at the top, until they transfer it to coolers strapped on the mules. Once they reach the bottom, the food goes straight into the freezers."

"Wait, where is the first deep freezer?"

"At the post office in Peach Springs on the rim of the canyon and probably the only post office in the country with a deep freezer. Although most of us have more important things delivered than ice cream sandwiches," Hope said.

"What could be more important than that?" Oz dropped his postcard into the satchel to be postmarked: 'Sent by mule from the bottom of Grand Canyon.' I wrote one for my parents.

"If you're done with your postcards, I have a surprise for you," Gran said. "We have reservations for the steak dinner at the Phantom Ranch Canteen."

"Do we have time to open the next clue before dinner?" I fished it out of my notebook:

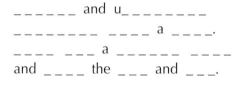

```
Y  T  H  E  B  G  X  X  W  H  O  E
Z  B  W  E  D  S  T  Q  U  A  A  M
T  O  G  E  T  H  E  R  I  N  P  R
W  E  F  U  P  A  N  D  A  D  W  A
E  U  O  N  F  H  K  C  A  F  I  Z
X  L  R  G  S  E  C  O  N  D  L  W
P  C  M  U  R  A  N  D  B  A  L  O
H  W  K  L  Q  E  Q  T  Z  G  O  N
R  N  T  A  I  T  F  I  N  D  W  K
T  C  I  T  G  F  H  D  S  F  U  I
O  O  M  E  O  K  O  J  K  N  T  J
O  N  E  S  T  T  O  W  H  Y  U  N
```

_ _ _ _ _ _ and u_ _ _ _ _ _ _ _

_ _ _ _ _ _ _ _ _ _ _ _ a _ _ _ _.

_ _ _ _ _ _ _ a _ _ _ _ _ _ _ _ _ _

and _ _ _ _ the _ _ _ and _ _ _.

"A puzzle. I love puzzles," Gran said. "*My* turn to solve one." We crowded around the bench where she sat and pointed out words as we found them. When we had a list, we organized them by length so that we could put them into the lines below the puzzle.

Why	Form	Second	Together
One	Find	Willow	
Who	Nest		
	Know		
	Clue		
	Time		

We filled in as many as we could and we were left with this:

Willow and u _ _ _ _ _ _ _ _ together form a clue.
Find one a second time and know the why and who.

"I don't understand. I have one extra word that doesn't fit. 'Nest.' And from the looks of these lines we are looking for a nine letter word that starts with 'u,'" Gran said.

I counted on my fingers. "Umbrellas," I said.

"Nice try, Nate. But that doesn't seem to be in the puzzle."

We found every 'u' in the puzzle and counted out nine letters to form words:

Urandbalo   Uonfhkcaf
Uqtsdewbz   Uwolliwpa
Utuwolliw   Upandadwa
Ufsdhfgti   Uiaandzns
                 Ungulates

"None of those are even words." Oz pushed his hair out of his eyes.

"Look again," Gran said. "I see one."

"Utuwolliw?" Kira said. "That's not a Havasupai word, is it, Hope?"

Hope shook her head. "I don't think so."

"Okay, then it must be 'ungulates.' But what does that even mean?" I asked.

"An ungulate is a hoofed mammal," Gran said.

"A hoofed mammal. Like a horse?"

"So we are looking for some willow trees near horses," Oz said.

"Are there even any horses down here?" I asked.

"No, but there are mules," Kira said. "That would be logical at Phantom Ranch."

"So keep your eyes open for willow near the mules when we are walking around tonight," I said.

The dinner bell that stands outside the Canteen rang at 5 p.m. People came from the cabins and the dormitories. Hikers who were soaking in the river hours before lined up outside the stone and wood building. A woman with a list called our name: "Wilder, party of five." We found our seating assignments for dinner.

Oz and I sat across from each other and the girls did the same. Gran got stuck with an old guy with a bushy white beard and a vest with pockets and zippers all over it. He introduced himself as Mike Strunk and said he was a photographer.

"A photographer? Kids, knowing photographers' crazy schedules, I bet Mr. Strunk is awake and breaking camp even earlier than we are," said Gran.

"Where have you been so far?" I spread our maps on the table next to me. Maybe he could help us.

"All over. I'm staying in the dorms and doing day hikes out to side canyons each day. What do you have there?" He glanced down at my notebook filled with ideas about the clues.

"Nate, don't bother Mr. Strunk with this," Gran said.

"It's no bother. It looks mighty interesting. Tell me about it." Mr. Strunk smiled.

I explained to him about Gramps, the hunt, and the clues we had managed to solve so far.

"But here's the one we're stuck on." I read him the clue about the bridges.

"Well, it says before the river make a decision." Your only option before the river is Clear Creek Trail. And obviously that leads down to a creek," he said.

"Thank you. That's what I've been telling these guys."

"But we have reservations at Indian Garden Campground, and Gramps knew we'd be heading that way," Kira said.

"This is only our first night here. Clear Creek could be a day trip from Phantom Ranch," I said.

"We hiked there yesterday," Mr. Strunk said. "Although we didn't go even close to the creek. That's 9 miles in. An 18-mile round trip is probably more than your grandfather was planning for you."

"Well thanks for the advice," I said.

"Of course. I'm truly impressed that the five of you are taking on this hike. I'll have to tell my grandson that it is possible for him to make it to the bottom."

"Well, we haven't made it back out, so don't build up his hopes just yet." Gran laughed.

About that time, they served dinner. The steak was juicy and the salty potatoes melted in my mouth. For dessert, they served chocolate cake. I pushed half of my piece across to Oz.

"Here, this is so you don't get hangry later," I said.

"Dude, you know me too well." Oz laughed and scooped the rest of the cake into his mouth in one bite.

I'VE ALWAYS BEEN AMAZED at how much food Oz can eat every day. Even after our dinner at the Canteen and then breakfast, he still wanted to buy cookies the next morning.

"Maybe we can wait until after we've figured out where to find willow at Phantom Ranch." I was never one to turn down cookies, but I was still full from our steak dinner.

Oz grinned. "Okay, but I'm holding you to that promise."

"I didn't promise anything. It was a suggestion."

"I know a promise of food when I hear it."

"Whatever, Oz, just keep your eyes open for willow."

"You mean like weeping willow trees? Those big ones we swing on at the pond?"

"I don't know, let's go find out."

Kira and Hope were in a deep discussion about ungulates as they followed us from our campsite. Gran decided to stay and read a book.

"Let's head for the corral," Kira said. "We think that's the best place to find ungulates since they could be horses or mules. I really like that word, 'ungulate.' It sounds so scientific."

Oz laughed so loud he probably woke up some other campers. "It reminds me of the sound someone makes when they're barfing."

I tried not to laugh. Both girls rolled their eyes.

The corral was across the creek and around the bottom half of the loop from the campground. It was busy because the wranglers were loading the mule train to head back up the South Kaibab Trail to the South Rim. The mules seemed anxious to go. They paced around and made noises just like in stories: *haaaaw-hee, haaaaw-hee.* Oz and I laughed every time one snorted.

Even though they were calmer than the one that took off with the kid on its back at Supai Tunnel, I didn't want to get too close to them. I rode a horse once and even though it was fun, big animals scare me a little.

Hope wasn't afraid at all. A mule came right over and let her pet its nose.

"How do you know so much about animals?" I asked.

Hope shrugged and kept stroking the mule who pushed its nose into her armpit. "What do you mean?"

"It's like you put a spell on that thing. You saw how mules acted around me the other day."

"That wasn't you, silly. That was the deer that scared him. You just have to be calm. Look, give me your hand."

She gently placed my hand on the mule's nose. It felt like soft velvet and his breath was hot on my fingers. She handed me three sugar cubes.

"Where did you get those?"

"From one of the wranglers. Now hold your hand flat and he'll take the sugar. Slow, steady, and calm. Don't always rush things." She smiled at me. I wondered if she was really talking about me rushing us into all of our decisions. She put the sugar cube on my palm and the mule pulled its lips away from its teeth and grabbed it gently. I tugged my hand away—slowly—and stuffed it in my pocket. I could still feel the heat from the mule's breath on my fingers.

"Well," I said. "These might be ungulates but I don't see any willow around here."

Just then, Kira and Oz came over. Oz waved a brochure in the air.

"You guys, they have a swimming pool here. We have to check it out," he said.

We followed him up the trail. "It's supposed to be just past the orchard." I didn't see much of an orchard, but there were some trees growing there in rows.

Hope stopped. "These are peach trees. They also grow near my house. The butterflies come every year to feast on them."

"No fruit trees. Swimming pool." Oz put an arm around each of us and Kira followed us. "It's supposed to be right here between cabin #4 and #5." There was a clearing in front of cabin #4 with a few boulders and shrubs.

"Oz, I don't see your swimming pool."

"Come on! I was so excited," he hung his head. Kira held up our guidebook and a page with two pictures side by side. One was labeled 1948 and showed a cabin in the background with a swimming pool in front of it. A man sat in a chair staring at the water. The picture next to it was labeled 2012. It showed the same cabin that stood in front of us and the same grassy area where we stood.

"Wait, I think some of the swimming pool is left." Kira walked over to a rock and stood on top of it. "It's the same rock that was in the middle of the pool in the first picture. If you had a time machine and could go back seventy years, you could go for swim."

"Funny! She's a funny girl, that cousin of yours." Oz glared at Kira.

I laughed and took the brochure from Kira. "The willow grow near the pond at the park. Maybe they grow near the river. Let's look down at Boat Beach." I showed them where it was on our map.

"Sounds good to me. If I can't swim, I can at least go to the beach," said Oz.

We followed the signs to Boat Beach, which was an actual beach with sand. I was surprised since I'd read that most of the Colorado River's shores were rocky or covered with shrubs. The water was also calm and shallow compared to the river's many rapids.

There was a group of rafts lined up along the shore. People loaded supplies into them. By this time, we were all hot and grumpy. Oz and Kira dragged their feet in the sand and refused to leave.

"Let's go back to the camp. The only way to cool off when it's like this is to go for a swim," Hope said.

We found Gran sitting on a rock under the shade of a tree with her feet in the water. Of course, she was reading a book.

"You guys having fun?" she asked.

"Actually, no. We're stuck on this clue, and had no luck at all," I handed the paper to her. "Do you know what willow looks like?"

"Nate, you should have asked me two hours ago. Of course I do. Did you forget what I did for a living? Did you look near the water? Willows like water. Like these." She pointed to the bushes we walked through at the edge of the creek when we left camp that morning.

"You're kidding? The willow was right here?"

She nodded. "I'm afraid so. These are coyote willow. They grow along the banks of rivers, creeks, and streams."

"Ponds, too?" Oz asked.

"Sometimes."

I kicked off my shoes and walked through the water to the tall shrubs on the other side of the creek. The branches were reddish and flexible and had skinny green leaves.

"Okay, so here are the willow, but what about the ungulates?"

"That's another story. I'm a botanist, not an equestrian specialist. Have you asked a ranger?"

We set off in search of a ranger and found Ranger Jeff, who came to Brian's rescue the day before. He stood near a circle of benches not far from the Canteen. A crowd of people were leaving like a meeting had just ended.

"Ranger Jeff? How is Brian? Is he okay?"

"He's going to be fine. Your quick thinking saved him. He spent some time in our medical facility yesterday afternoon and his group was heading back out last night."

"They were going to run?"

117

"No…walking this time…and with plenty of hydration."

"That's good. We need your help. Can you tell us where to find some willow near the mules down here in Phantom Ranch?" I asked.

"Willow by the mules, huh? Where did you get that idea?"

I handed him the clue and he read it silently. He shook his head and grinned.

"Well. Whoever wrote this may be guiding you down a slightly different path. You could consider the mules, or might I suggest you come to my ranger talk at four o'clock this afternoon? You might learn something." He handed the paper back to me.

Oz stomped away and punched the air in front of him. I thanked Ranger Jeff and ran to catch up with Oz.

"You *could* consider the mules? That guy was laughing at us. Gramps knew good and well that mules don't hang out by the willows. Maybe he just used that word, ungulates, because he wanted to sound poetic. That Gramps of yours, a regular Edgar Allan Poe of Grand Canyon."

"Take it easy, Oz. Let's go back to the mule corral. Maybe we missed something."

Oz stopped dead in his tracks, folded his arms, and glared at me.

"No. This is stupid. We've walked all over this ranch. This clue has nothing to do with mules and willows or horses and willows. It's the wrong animal. Even the willow itself is coyote willow. I think Gramps sent us on a wild goose chase. You know how every one of his treasure hunts had a false clue in it? I think he's sitting up there in heaven laughing at us."

"Oz, don't talk about Gramps that way." Kira clenched her teeth.

"I'm sorry, Kira, he was a great guy and I wish he was here with us. I love a good treasure hunt as much as the next guy, but we aren't going to find our answers here."

"We don't know that," I said. "We might find out something at Ranger Jeff's presentation and maybe even more when we head up to Clear Creek Trail tomorrow."

"Didn't you hear me? No. I'm not going to your stupid ranger presentation, and there's no way I'm going with you to Clear Creek Trail again. I'm sick and tired of following you around everywhere. Gramps might not have been crazy, but you are."

I was stunned. I stared at Oz. "I know that Clear Creek has to be the right way to go."

"Nate, you're my best friend, but you don't know which temple, you don't know which trail, and you don't know everything. Let someone else make a decision for a change. Let someone else have an opinion, would you?" Oz stomped off and left me standing in the trail.

Kira wiped tears from her eyes as she and Hope turned to follow Oz.

I HURRIED AFTER KIRA AND HOPE, but what I really wanted to do was tackle Oz as he stomped off down the path. He had a lot of nerve, making Kira cry and calling Gramps crazy. Plus, down deep I was afraid what Oz said might be true.

The girls sat on a bench near the ranger station, and I collapsed next to Kira.

"What if he's right, Nate? What if this is all for nothing?" Kira said. "Maybe Gramps just created this whole adventure to make you feel good. I got all of his attention last year because of my science project, and now he's giving you this hunt."

"If he wanted to give me something, he would make sure it had a solution. He knew how much I hate looking for things that aren't there." I threw my notebook on the ground.

Hope had been quiet, with her arm around Kira. She stared at the painted lady butterflies on the peach trees behind us.

"Isn't that the point?" she asked and turned to look at me.

"What?"

"Gramps said in the letter that sometimes you find the best things when you aren't looking for them. Even if we don't solve the clues, this is still the greatest adventure of our lives, and we're on it together. And don't forget about Gran. She thought this was important enough to leave home right after Gramps died and take the four of us with her. You can tell she's still sad, just like my grandmother when my grandfather died. We need to do this for Gran, too."

I felt like someone had punched me in the gut. She was right: the treasure hunt didn't really matter, except it did to me because it was the last thing I had from Gramps.

After Kira finally calmed down, we went into the Canteen. Gran was inside playing cards with Mr. Strunk and two other people from his photography tour.

"Where's Oz? I figured he would be in here with you," I said.

"When I passed him on the path, he was on his way to camp. Did something happen between you two? He looked pretty upset."

I nodded.

We went straight back to our campsite and tried to coax Oz out of the tent.

"It's 90 degrees. You're going to turn into dehydrated Oz jerky," I said, but there was only silence. I unzipped the door and the smell of stinky gym socks and rotten eggs filled my nose.

"We need to wash some clothes. It's getting rank in these tents. Oz, if you won't come out, at least toss me your rope and our laundry."

Dusty red socks and dirty t-shirts flew one by one out of the tent. This laundry cyclone was followed by a neatly wound coil of rope.

"Thanks. I knew you'd have some rope in there."

"It's not rope; it's parachute cord. Every good outdoors man has some parachute cord."

At least he was talking to me. I'd give Oz some time to pout in silence, and then I was sure he'd be back to his normal self. I pulled the remaining sugar cubes from my pocket and slid them through the door of the tent.

"Peace offering, man. Maybe you just need some sugar."

The girls helped me string the parachute cord from the picnic table to the T-bar where our backpacks hung to make a clothesline. We hauled our dirty clothes down to the creek, and dunked them in the water. We couldn't use soap in the creek, but we rubbed our clothes on rocks and hoped the smell would disappear.

"I've been thinking more about the legend." Kira handed me a blue t-shirt, and I folded it over the laundry line. "We definitely need to include the ringtail eating our food and finding Brian passed out in the middle of nowhere."

"What about the lizard in Gran's tent?" Hope wrung out a pair of socks and sniffed them. "Smells clean enough to me."

"I like those ideas. Will you help me write more tonight?" I asked.

"Sure. But…why are we writing this?" Kira said.

A breeze blew and a wet sock flapped against my cheek. "I don't know. For fun? As a journal of our trip? Of course, it's just like Gramps' hunt. We might not know the why until we get to the end."

When it was time to head to Ranger Jeff's presentation, Oz was still in the tent and wouldn't talk to us. There were already twelve people seated in the circle of benches when we got there. Kira, Hope, and I squeezed into the front row and waited for Ranger Jeff to show up. His baseball hat and green shorts bobbed around the corner. He tipped his hat when he saw us. He leaned a chalkboard against a tree and cleared his throat.

"Stones and bones. The history of Grand Canyon is filled with these two things," he said. "Tonight, we are talking about the archaeology, anthropology, and geology of the canyon. When I was a kid," he motioned to us, "one of my favorite things to do was dig in the dirt. It wasn't until I was grown that I realized that digging in the dirt had taught me more about the mysteries of life than simply how quickly my mom could throw me in the bathtub. The dirt and rocks around us…how they got here and who lived on them…tell us the story of the canyon."

Ranger Jeff spent an hour talking about this stuff. We pushed aside piles of pine needles to find artifacts he had buried. Oz would love these piles of pine needles. I wished he was here with us.

Sticky pine sap covered my hands, and I was beginning to feel that Ranger Jeff had only invited us because he wanted a big crowd at his presentation. Just when I was ready to leave, Ranger Jeff handed two brown pipe cleaners to each of us. We got an instruction sheet filled with step-by-step pictures to create an animal that looked like the llama that lives down the street from Gran and Gramps' house.

Ranger Jeff showed us how to bend the pipe cleaners in half, bend the back legs down, and then make a front leg. We wrapped the extra pipe cleaner around itself to make coils on the legs. Then we made a head by bending the other half of the pipe cleaner forward and back around the neck.

I kept dropping the pipe cleaners, and Kira's kept coming unwound. Hope's hands, though, moved fast, and before I knew it she was making a second animal.

"How did you get so good at making these llamas?" I teased.

"It's not a llama, it's a horse." She wrapped and tucked to create a second one.

"A horse. How do you know?"

Hope shushed me because Ranger Jeff was explaining that we were making split-twig figures like those found under rock cairns in the back of caves throughout Grand Canyon.

"Archaeologists have carbon dated these figures between 2900 BC and 1250 BC, also known as the Late Archaic Period. We believe the split-twig figures were made to honor the spirit of the animals before a hunt. They are likely deer or bighorn sheep, our resident ungulates, or large, hooved mammals in the canyon." Ranger Jeff looked right at me when he said the word ungulate.

So, that's what an ungulate really was.

"Has anyone ever seen these before?" he asked.

Three people, including Hope, raised their hands. The first two said they saw pictures of them in the Visitor Center when they arrived at the park.

"And what about you?" Ranger Jeff nodded at Hope.

"My grandmother taught me to make them. But we don't use pipe cleaners."

"What do you use?"

"My uncle collects willow branches from along Supai Creek, and soaks them in water. Then he splits them down the middle with a sharp rock. That's why they're called split-twig figurines."

The word willow echoed in my ears. Willow and ungulate. Hope hesitated but raised her hand again.

"But we don't think they are bighorn sheep," she said. I was surprised at how brave she was to disagree with the ranger.

"No?" he asked.

"No, we make split-twig horses—to celebrate how much

the horse means to us. Horses and mules carry all our supplies down the trail to our home in Supai." Hope hadn't stopped making her split-twig figures and a pile was starting to form in front of her.

"That's very appropriate. The horse, and the mules, actually, are other 'ungulates' that we celebrate in modern times. Not because we hunt them for food, but because they so graciously bear our loads into and out of the canyon. If not for those animals, Phantom Ranch wouldn't exist and the people of Supai would have a much harder way of life." Ranger Jeff smiled.

The girls walked in front of me down the trail to our campsite. "Why didn't you tell us before about the willow," Kira asked Hope.

"I didn't even think about it. I haven't made them since I was six. But once I had those pipe cleaners in my hands, it all started coming back to me."

I pushed past the girls. This was the answer to Gramps' riddle, but the clue said: 'Find one a second time and know the why and who.' I just knew we would find those split-twig figures for a second time along Clear Creek Trail. I was excited to tell Gran and Oz about our discovery and to convince them that I was right.

When we arrived back at camp, Oz and Gran were eating dinner: sandwiches from the extra sack lunches we bought at the Canteen. Gran had the map spread out on the picnic table and they were tracing routes with their fingers.

Oz and I locked eyes. He raised his eyebrows and handed me a sugar cube, one that I shoved into the tent before we left for the presentation.

"Peace offering?" he asked. "I was frustrated and hungry, and I shouldn't have said those things about Gramps. I've always known that Gran is a wise one. She gave me a talking to and a sandwich. Good combination."

The sugar cube melted in my mouth as I sat down next to Oz. No matter how many fights Oz and I had, we always stayed friends. "Peace. We have news. We found the willow and the mule, which is actually not a mule, but a bighorn sheep."

Kira and I explained what we had learned at the presentation and showed them our pipe cleaner animals.

"And Hope was a whiz at making them," Kira said. "Show Gran and Oz yours."

Hope blushed and handed them her horses.

"These are so cool," Oz said. "Could I keep one, you know like a souvenir from our trip?"

Hope nodded.

"I would kind of like to see a real one made from willow," I said.

"Well, we can do that," Gran said. She picked up a dead willow twig floating in the water, tied Oz's rope around it, secured it to the leg of our picnic table, and let the line out into the creek. "This can soak tonight, and we'll split it in the morning."

"Gran and I are dizzy looking at all of these trails," Oz said. "We thought opening another clue might help us."

I had been so excited, I forgot all about the next clue. When I unfolded the piece of paper, there was a hand-drawn picture:

The drawing had a horizontal line at the bottom with six

circles arching over it. The circle on the far right was small and shaded black on the right side. Each circle grew bigger and the fourth one—at the top of the arch—was a white circle. There was no shading, but it had a black dot in the very center and four thick lines on the top, bottom, left, and right of the circle. The fifth and sixth circles grew smaller and had black shading on the left side. Where a seventh circle should have completed the arc, there was an empty space.

Below it was one sentence:

Travel as if you are waking up.

"Is there a note or anything?" Kira asked.

I checked inside the envelope. "Nope. That's it."

"It reminds me of the phases of the moon, like on a calendar," Hope said. Hope was right. My calendar at home had shaded half circles and full circles just like this.

"But aren't the phases of the moon usually in a full circle around the earth?" Kira grabbed a pen and drew in my notebook. She sketched a circle in the center, labeled it earth, and scratched eight shaded circles around it.

"And look at this." Oz pointed to the white circle at the top of Gramps' clue. "This looks like the symbol on the New Mexico license plate."

As kids, Oz and I always found license plates during long car trips. I remembered the blue license plate with the yellow symbol in the middle.

"So does Gramps want us to go to New Mexico? I don't

think that's anywhere near the trails in Grand Canyon," Oz said.

"No, these circles aren't the phases of the moon. It's the phases of the sun. Look it's rising in the east." I pointed to the right side of the paper and traced my finger over the arch, "and setting in the west. Travel as if you are waking up. The sun is waking up in the east. I told you we needed to go east."

The group stared at me. Kira was the first to speak. "Nate, the picture says 'travel as if you are waking up.' When the sun is waking up it travels west. I'm pretty sure this means we need to head west."

I suddenly felt hot. I pulled my fingers into fists and took a deep breath.

"I'm sorry, and I know you all think I don't let anyone else have an opinion, but I know that you're wrong. This is clearly EAST."

"Nate, honey, I don't think that Gramps would send us to Indian Garden and then have us head back this direction to Clear Creek," Gran said.

"No, he wouldn't and if you guys had listened to me, we wouldn't have wasted a day looking for willows. We would have already found what we're looking for."

"What *are* we looking for, Nate?" asked Kira. "A nest? A nest of what? We have no idea what we're searching for. There are temples and towers and buttes all along these routes, and who knows where there is a nest or another split-twig figure. This is like finding a needle in a haystack."

Hope twirled her bracelet and spoke in a voice louder

than I'd ever heard from her. "We aren't going to fix this by arguing. I didn't know Gramps as well as the rest of you, but I don't think he would have wanted us getting mad at each other."

Gran nodded.

"Nate," Hope said now in her normal quiet way, "all along we've been voting. It's only fair. You said it yourself."

"All in favor of leaving for Indian Garden in the morning and heading west?" Kira asked. Gran, Oz, Hope, and Kira raised their hands.

"All opposed?"

"Don't, Kira. I get it. I'm the only one opposed." I crawled into the tent and listened to them plan our route without me.

THE SUN WASN'T EVEN UP, but I could feel the minutes ticking away before we would head west—the wrong direction. I put on my boots as quietly as possible and slid out of the tent with my flashlight and water bottle. This was the last chance I had. I would go to Clear Creek alone.

Thankfully Oz is a heavy sleeper, so he didn't even move when I tripped on the willow twig in front of the tent. Gran, or someone, had split the twig and the two halves bowed out in the shape of a V. It was 3:51 a.m. I knew that hikers would be packing up camp or cooking breakfast before 5 a.m., so I needed to make a break for it before everyone woke up.

My headlamp threw a circle of light just in front of my feet as I trudged across the creek. I'd read that twilight is an hour and half before the sun rises, so the sky would lighten up soon.

I walked up the trail toward the intersection of Bright Angel Creek and the Colorado River. Something rustled to my right. My flashlight lit up the face of a mule deer, the same type we saw earlier in the week. It munched on grass

near the banks of the river.

A sound above us caught my attention. It was like the wind blowing in short strong bursts. The noise stopped for a few seconds and then started again. The deer must have heard it too because she looked up. So did I, but I couldn't see anything but darkness and faint hints of light from the eastern sky. The deer seemed curious and followed the noise down the trail to the east. Call me crazy, but like the deer, I had to find out what was puffing above me.

We, the deer and I, followed the trail in the direction of Boat Beach. I stayed ten feet behind so I wouldn't scare her off. The noise stopped completely, but the deer kept walking. I was a little nervous about setting off for Clear Creek Trail in the dark, so I figured following the deer until it got light wouldn't hurt. At the turn off to Boat Beach, she headed to the left up to a new area I hadn't been. The silhouette of the Black Bridge appeared as the sun rose behind it.

Next to me were the remains of a pueblo along the river. There were four or five rooms divided by scattered stone walls and a round kiva in the middle of the site. The split willow was still in my hand so I wrapped it like Ranger Jeff taught us. I wondered if people sat in their houses here on the riverbanks when they made these stick animals 4,000 years ago. The willow branch was even harder to wrap than the pipe cleaners had been, but I stuck with it and finally had an animal with a long neck and coils around it. The legs stuck out to the side though, more like wings than legs. In fact, it looked like a condor, with its ring of feathers around its neck. Kira would laugh but I think she'd agree that it could be a condor.

The sound was right above us now. I squinted and saw a large black bird. The deer looked back at me as if to say, "Are we okay with this huge thing swooping down on us." I nodded and peered up again. Probably another turkey vulture. It circled and glided—down low and then high again. After another flap of its wings, it flew off behind me. I turned and watched for the wobble, but it flattened its wings into a straight line and followed the Colorado River to the west. No wobble at all. It was a condor.

What was a condor doing down here near the river? Was it following me or maybe the deer? It circled to get our attention and then flew away to the west. It traveled like the waking sun. Maybe the bird was trying to tell me something. The others were right: we needed to move like the waking sun and head west.

Ranger Jeff had talked about celebrating the spirits of the animals. Maybe it wasn't a condor I'd seen, but it didn't matter. I was celebrating the spirit of the animal that had just shown me the path we needed to take. I thought about leaving my split-twig condor on the floor of one of the pueblo's rooms, but I remembered the 'Leave No Trace' motto I lectured Oz about, so I kept it with me. I ran back to camp. It was 5:15 on my watch.

Gran was already awake and reading at the table with a cup of coffee.

"Nate, where did you come from?"

"Just down there. I needed to figure things out."

"And?"

"And, you were all right. We need to follow the path of the sun, which means heading west. Now, we just need to figure out where."

Gran stood up and gave me a hug. "Looks like the vote was fair after all. Amazing what an early morning walk can do to clear your head."

After another stop in the Canteen for bagels and as many sack lunches as they would sell us, we broke camp and put our packs on our backs. We hadn't dropped any weight, but my pack felt lighter because we were getting closer to solving the clues. Before that, though, we had to make it 4.7 miles to Indian Garden Campground.

With our arguments behind us, the hike was fun. We crossed the giant Bright Angel suspension bridge with the girls and Gran in the lead. Our feet banged on the metal flooring, and about halfway across I didn't hear Oz. When I turned around, he was stopped in the middle of the bridge staring back at Phantom Ranch.

"Yo, Oz. What's up?" I crept up close to him.

"Nothing."

"No seriously, are you okay. Are you still mad at me?"

"No. It's just that now that we're leaving, and heading up—ugh, I can't even think about that—I don't know if I'll ever be back in the bottom of Grand Canyon."

I knew exactly how he felt. After the bridge, we walked for over a mile through some sand dunes. I imagined the rushing river pushing the sand up on the walls of the canyon. It was tough going, trudging through the sand.

The River Resthouse, our first landmark, was a stone building like a small pavilion where we sat in the shade and drank our water. Then we followed Pipe Creek up the canyon. Its walls towered above us.

Around a corner, we stared up at the Devil's Corkscrew. It looked like we would make a hundred turns before we made it out. It was still early, so most of the trail was shaded and we climbed hard. I watched Gran's trekking poles dig in with each step she took.

A million switchbacks later, we cleared the corkscrew and stood on a plateau of flat rocks stacked on top of each other.

"We have to be getting close, right?" Oz walked into the creek on our right and splashed water on his face.

"This is Garden Creek. It will lead us straight to Indian Garden." Hope smiled and jumped up and down.

"How do you know? Have you been here before?" Oz asked.

"Yes, but I was really little. I don't remember much about it. My dad and my uncle used to hike across the Tonto Plateau to Indian Garden every fall, though."

"Some sort of Havasupai tradition?" Oz asked.

"Sort of. My great, great grandfather was named Billy Burro. He and his wife lived at Indian Garden until 1928. They grew all kinds of crops like corn and beans. That's why it's called Indian *Garden*. My dad thought it was important to visit the spot where my family lived before this became a national park."

I looked at the canyon in front of us. At the end was a sheer red cliff jam-packed with switchbacks, and the rest of the valley was filled with shady trees. I could understand why Hope's ancestors chose this place to live.

The campsite at Indian Garden was on our right. It was much smaller than Bright Angel Campground. Each site had a wooden awning over a picnic table. There were curvy gravel paths with tall plants growing along the edges so our campsite felt hidden. We set up our tents on either side of the awning and filled up our water bottles to cool off. I was anxious to open the last clue. I tore open the envelope and read:

Clue #5 will lead Clue #7 to the point where #2 can be seen Clue #1 is behind so make sure your eyes are keen. Within a crevice find Clue #6 I left for you to see and right above I hope you see Clue #4 and then Clue #3.

"Finally, he gives us something that makes sense," Oz said.

"That's a lot to sort out. Where's your notebook, Nate?" I handed it to Kira.

"I'll read it again and you fill in the answers we already know."

"? TRAIL will lead WEST to the point where ? ROCK FORMATION can be seen. REDWALL LIMESTONE is behind so make sure your eyes are keen. Within a crevice find a SPLIT-TWIG FIGURE, I left for you to see, And right above I hope you see a NEST and then a ? SOUND?"

"How can we see a sound?" Oz disappeared into our tent and came out with his hand-crank battery charger. He plugged in his phone and turned the handle.

"Ugh. I'm going to sneak in your tent and steal that crank tonight. I can't listen to a recording of you snoring again. Haven't you got anything else?" Kira asked.

"Sure, I've made recordings every night. Even last night when Nate snuck out." I thought he had been asleep.

"Sorry I woke you."

"No, it's cool. I'm glad you got things figured out."

"One thing I don't have figured out is what waterway we're looking for," I said.

"That's right, Clue #5 did say something about a waterway. Now that we're all in agreement that we're heading west, let's check the map again," said Kira.

We spread all of the clues out on the table and poured over the map.

"There is only one main trail from here, the Tonto Trail." I traced my finger along the long winding route to the west.

"Yeah, but it goes on forever, how will we know where to stop?" Hope asked.

"Well, we know we're looking for a temple, pyramid, tower, or butte that will show us the way." I flipped the pages back to my list of rock formations and crossed off Brahma, Deva, and Zoroaster, since they were all to the east. "That leaves us with Horus, the Tower of Set, Cheops Pyramid, and way down here," I slid my finger to the bottom of the list, "Osiris Temple and the Tower of Ra."

Kira whispered under her breath and unfolded her fingers. "That's six different formations. How will we know?"

Gran sat at the end of the table and stared thoughtfully at the map.

"Maybe we should head out to Plateau Point tonight? This map makes it look like we can see several of these formations from there, and I hear the sunsets are amazing."

We left at 6:30 to see the sunset and hopefully figure out which rock formation Gramps wanted us to see. We gave ourselves an hour for the mile and a half trek to Plateau Point.

I heard the roar of the Colorado River before I saw it, and suddenly we were staring down 1,600 feet at the green water below. To our left and down the canyon, the water turned white from a rapids section. I thought about those rafters we saw at Boat Beach and wondered how far down the river they were now, two days later. To our right a metal tripod sat on the very tip of Plateau Point but a camera wasn't attached to it, and I didn't see its owner.

"Now, who do you suppose that belongs to?" Gran asked.

I walked over to the tripod and peered down at another ledge below the main drop-off. On it stood a hefty man in a brown vest and wearing a cowboy hat. In his hands, was a camera.

I knew immediately who it was. "Hi, Mr. Strunk," I said.

He stopped and shaded his eyes to look up at me.

"Nate. How are you? I've been thinking about you kids. I'll be up in a second."

He put his camera around his neck and climbed hand over hand up the layers of grayish rock. Finally, he threw his leg over the edge and pulled himself up.

"I've done that a time or two. Good to see you." He stuck out his hand and shook mine firmly. By this time, Gran and the rest of the crew had noticed the rock climbing Santa Claus.

"Mr. Strunk, what are you doing here?" Kira asked.

"Just snapping a few test shots before the big sunset show starts. I'm staying at Indian Garden for two nights."

"We're doing the same thing. We're thinking about a day

hike on the Tonto Trail tomorrow, and then we hike out on Thursday," Kira said.

"The Tonto? I was out there early this morning. Want to look at some pictures?" He turned his camera so we could see the digital screen on the back.

Mr. Strunk pushed the button and flipped through his pictures slowly. Each one showed different views into the canyon, and many had rock formations with the sun rising behind them. It must have been about the same time the deer and I were being eyed for morning breakfast.

"Wait, would you go back?" I asked. He pushed the left arrow about five pictures back.

The screen was filled with a rock formation. It looked like someone set a replica of the Great Pyramids of Egypt on top of a tall base. A rectangular white stone perched at the very tip of the red pyramid.

"What is that?"

"That's Cheops Pyramid. You'll get a great view from the Tonto tomorrow. Why?"

I knelt down and pulled the clues and Gramps' letter from my backpack. All along I'd been wondering about the sketches at the top of the letter. I didn't know if Gramps was just recording memories of the canyon or if they had more meaning. I should have known he would never put something down in writing for no reason. I examined each doodle closely.

"There are six rock formations at the top of the letter. I thought they were just for illustration, but maybe one of them matches Cheops Pyramid." I pointed at the drawings.

"Did you see the numbers?" Kira asked.

Dear Kids,

Welcome to the Grand Canyon. By now you've peered down from the South Rim and had your first glimpse of the glories that await you. But the rim is only the tip of the iceberg. There are mysteries waiting to be discovered within the canyon that are far greater than anything you could imagine.

We've been planning this trip for more than a year. I wish I were there with you, but there is a way we can still experience the Grand Canyon together. Do you remember how I loved to create treasure hunts? Think of this as my last one—specifically designed for the four of you. At the end, is a treasure far greater than any I've given you before.

All of you have an important role in this adventure. Nate, you see yourself as a navigator; Kira—a scientist; Oz—a survivalist; and Hope—a naturalist. These qualities lie within each of you. Rely on these talents, but more importantly, rely on each other. All it takes is the ability to open your minds and follow the clues that Mother Nature (and I) have provided.

Why am I doing this? I have spent much of my life alone studying the Grand Canyon, and it is time for you to experience the things I learned. Have patience. I hope you will find the discovery of a lifetime.

Look, listen, be observers of all things beautiful, scary, and mysterious. Rely on your senses and document your thoughts, as even a seemingly obscure one may be the answer to what you seek.

Let's get going! Your first step is to find my friend Kelly Bartlett. Kelly holds the keys to your exploration. Your hard work will be worth it because the next generation needs to understand the mysteries this treasure holds as much as you do.

I love you all.

Gramps

P.S. There is a quote by the poet Carl Sandburg: "For each man sees himself in the Grand Canyon—each one makes his own canyon before he comes, each one brings and carries away his own canyon." I have no doubt that you will each carry away your own canyon and will be changed forever.

P.P.S. Be safe—You are undertaking a bold journey fraught with uncertainty.

"What numbers?" Oz nudged me over to see the paper. "Each one of these sketches has a number squiggled into the line drawing. And check out the one with the number 2." Kira tapped the one on the right margin of the letter.

I squinted my eyes like Hope had taught me in order to pick up on the changes in the contours. Then I looked out into the canyon and back to Mr. Strunk's camera.

"#2 is the outline of Cheops Pyramid. They look identical."

"Big deal, there are five others on here. What's so important about number 2?" Oz asked.

"Nate's right, remember the clue?" Kira pulled the clues from my notebook and read.

"'Clue #5 will lead you to the point where #2 can be seen.' He dropped the word 'clue' before the number. We just assumed Gramps was talking about the second clue. He was, but he was also telling us exactly which rock formation it was. He wanted us to find these numbers hidden in his sketches and figure it out." Kira hugged me so hard she knocked off her glasses.

This was what we had been waiting for. We knew where we were going, and we knew what we were looking for. I dropped my daypack on the rocks beside me, set aside my notebook, and unfolded the map on the ground. Two men approached Mr. Strunk. They must have been part of his photography group because I heard a discussion of lenses and filters.

Kira was the first to find our rock formation on the map: Cheops Pyramid. It was across the Colorado River but we estimated you could see it from Horn Creek or Salt Creek, three miles west on the Tonto Trail. The creeks were two squiggly blue lines on the map.

"How will be know which creek?" Hope asked.

"I think we'll know when we get there," Kira said.

"I hope it's Horn Creek, since it's the first one we'll come to. It would be awesome to have an easy hiking day before we head back up to the rim," Oz said.

The sun had set behind the rocks to the west, and the sky was turning a pinkish-gray. I knew it would be getting dark soon and we had a mile and a half to our camp.

"Let's head back so we can get an early start tomorrow." I tossed the map into my pack, and we headed out.

The trail was harder to navigate because it was getting dark and we didn't have our flashlights. I rolled my ankle trying to avoid the fresh mule bombs from the pack train that must have walked to Plateau Point in the afternoon. Hope taught us to walk on the edge of the trail to prevent dust clouds and the ankle turns. We angled our feet inward, balanced on the walls on either side of the ruts and tried to avoid the prickly pear cactus that lined the trail. I'm sure we looked like ducks.

When we arrived at camp, there was just enough time to work on our legend before we went to sleep. I unbuckled my pack and unloaded the water bottles, a rain jacket, and an energy bar that was squished into a sticky ball. After I put the map on the table, I reached in for my notebook where our legend was written, but there was nothing left in the pack.

"My notebook with Gramps' letter and all of the clues," I yelled, "they're gone!"

"WHAT DO YOU MEAN GONE?"
Kira asked. I unzipped every pocket on my backpack and dumped it upside down.

"Whoa, dude. You're freaking out. What's wrong?" Oz asked.

"My notebook, all the clues, Gramps' letter…everything is gone." I shook the backpack again.

"Slow down, Nate," Gran said. "Have you checked in your tent?"

"No, I haven't let it out of my sight the whole trip. That has everything in it." I crawled into the tent and tossed our sleeping bags onto the ground outside.

"Hold on, killer. Notebook or no notebook, we don't want to be sleeping with scorpions in our bags tonight," Oz picked up the sleeping bags and folded them across our picnic table.

"When did you last see it?" Hope knelt in the opening of the tent.

"I don't know. I had the map at Plateau Point. Kira and I were looking at Cheops Pyramid, and…" My mind went blank. It was like wandering around blind. The last time

I remember holding my notebook was at camp before we headed down the trail. I tore out of the tent and threw the sleeping bags off the picnic table.

"Seriously, Nate. I mean it about the scorpions. We'll find it. Just calm down," Oz said. "Kira, did you see the notebook when you and Nate were looking at the map?"

Kira closed her eyes and stood motionless. Her eyes popped open.

"You took it out of your pack before the map and set it on a rock. I remember seeing it there."

I breathed a sigh of relief. As Kira described it, it was like watching someone else. I could see myself set the notebook on the ground. I looked at my watch: 9:04 p.m.

"We have to get it." I tossed the sleeping bags into the tent and fished through the mesh pockets for my headlamp. "Oz, fill up the water bottles, we have to go back for it."

"We have to go back? You mean you and me? Can't we just get it tomorrow? Nobody is going to be out there to take it. Besides who would want your notebook anyway?" Oz plopped down on the bench.

"I'll go with you, Nate." Hope retied the laces on her hiking boots and strapped a headlamp on her head. "The others can stay here. We'll be back before you know it."

"Hope, that's very sweet of you to offer," Gran said, "but you know how I feel about this—"

"We're not splitting up!" we all said together.

"That's right. It's all of us tonight or we wait until morning," Gran said.

"But what if it rains tonight. Everything will be ruined." I looked desperately at Oz.

"Let's vote," Kira said matter-of-factly. I was so tired of voting. I know it had been my idea, but I made a note not to suggest voting again on this trip.

"Everybody who thinks we should go back tonight?" I threw my hand up in the air. Hope raised hers just as fast. I looked back and forth from Kira to Oz, both of whom had their arms crossed. But Oz must have felt sorry for me. He sighed and slowly raised his hand.

"Alright. Thank you. Let's get moving."

Exhausted, we geared up again, and started down the path out of camp. Our headlamps lit up the trail in front of us. I was careful to look directly in front of me to step over any roots or loose rocks. Ten minutes down the trail, a bright light blinded us. Someone was coming from the other direction.

Voices and laughter drifted through the otherwise quiet night. We stopped to let whoever was on the trail pass.

"Just the people I was looking for."

My headlamp shone on a white beard and a jolly smile—Mr. Strunk.

"I thought you might be missing this, Nate." He waved a blue notebook in the air and then handed it to me.

"Thank you so much. Where did you find it?" I clutched it to my chest.

"You left so quickly, I didn't even get to say goodbye. I found it on a rock. I recognized it from our steak dinner when you showed me your clues."

"Mr. Strunk, you're a hero. You just saved us a scary trek in the dark back out to Plateau Point. I vote that Mr. Strunk makes a special appearance in our legend. Super Strunk, greatest of all super heroes," Oz said.

"It's not a comic book story, Oz." We all laughed.

"Have a good night," Mr. Strunk said as he and his friends moved past us and headed for their campsite.

"Are you okay now?" Hope asked.

I nodded. "Thanks for agreeing so quickly to go back to Plateau Point with me."

"We're like a team, right?" Hope raised her hand. "High five?"

Hope always made a face when Oz and I high-fived—like she thought it was lame—so I was surprised she wanted to do it. We all stepped forward and touched her hand.

"I'd like to say something on this momentous occasion, mates," Oz said in his best Australian accent. "We, my friends, are like the four musketeers…and Gran. It's all for one and one for all."

"There weren't four musketeers," Kira said to Oz.

We laughed and talked all the way back to our campsite. Even though Oz's speech was kind of dumb, he had a point. We had become a team. And a team needs a calm leader. I took a deep breath. In the morning, our team would embark on our final mission to find Gramps' treasure.

The sun rose, and I made sure to put my notebook safely in my daypack as we got ready to leave on our hike. According to the map, we would walk a total of five to six miles round trip. I wrote out a list and asked everyone to make sure they had the right things packed: first aid kit, rain gear, extra clothes, headlamps, extra food, and water. There was no drinking water along the trail, so we filled up every bottle we had.

Our path was the same one we had taken the night before to Plateau Point, except we veered west at a sign for the Tonto Trail. After a few minutes, we could see the Battleship rock formation. This was the place we saw the ranger with her radio telemetry equipment from the South Rim. There were clouds in the sky, but the sun was still shining. We found some shade under a boulder and sat down for a water break.

Kira paced and looked through her binoculars, her eyes glued to the Battleship.

"Come sit in the shade, Kira. You're going to give yourself heat stroke," Gran said.

"I'm fine. Besides, I can't see as well over there." Kira lowered her binoculars to look at Gran, but raised them again quickly.

"What are you looking for? Obviously, condors. Like you spend every minute of your day doing, but what specifically. Are you just willing one to fly up in the sky?" Oz asked and passed me some Gatorade powder, which I poured into my water bottle.

"There is a cave up there. Actually, there are lots of caves up there. It's where the condors gave birth to their young 10,000 years ago." She swung her head from side to side.

"I thought the condors were introduced to Grand Canyon after they became endangered. I didn't know they lived here all along," I said.

"That's the point. They lived here…in these rocks…for thousands of years. And then they gradually started dying out. When the captive breeding and reintroduction program started in the 1980s, the only condors left were in California. They starting breeding those and releasing them from Vermilion Cliffs every year. It's amazing that 10,000 years later, they still manage to find their way home." Kira fooled with the focus on her binoculars as if trying to get a clearer view of things.

"Hey, if you have a good cave, I say why not move back in even if you have to clear out some 10,000-year-old cobwebs," Oz said and we all laughed.

"There! I knew it was there. That has to be it. That has to be what we are looking for." Kira bounced on her toes. I stood up beside her and she handed me the binoculars.

"What do you mean?" I closed one eye and looked through the binoculars until I spotted the black hole that Kira pointed to on the side of the rock formation.

"We're on the right trail. If we're looking for a nest, there has to be one up there. I just know Gramps wants us to find a baby condor. The tracking list on the Grand Canyon website listed numbers 187 and 280 as nesting up there this year. We need to climb," she said.

I passed the binoculars to Oz, who looked and gave them to Hope.

"Kira, the Battleship has some very technical climbing, especially from this side. Do you see how sheer those cliff areas are at the top? Trust me, that route is ten times harder and more dangerous than anything I climb. Gramps would never expect you to endanger yourself. That looks like a climb for an expert. We just don't have the gear. Let's just stick to the trail—we must be looking for somewhere else," Gran said.

Oz put his arm around Gran. "Yeah, what she said. I vote for no climbing."

Kira didn't seem to like what she heard. She ignored Gran and scrambled up the rocks at the bottom of the wall and climbed over a sloped area.

"What are you doing, Kira?" I asked.

She slid her hands up a flat vertical section of rock and tucked her fingers into some cracks. She climbed like a monkey. Within seconds, she was higher than any of us could reach.

"Kira, come down from there. Right now!" Gran used her bossy voice again.

"If I can just get over to that ledge, I'll be close to the caves. I just know it." Kira continued to climb.

"Kids, get under her. All of us. If she falls, she's going

to break something. Kira Marie Wilder. Climb down from there this instant."

But my cousin seemed possessed. When she stopped for a few seconds, I thought she might have changed her mind, but she didn't. She eyed the rocks in front of her and found crevices for both her hands and feet so she could boost herself up higher. There was no way we could reach her even if Oz stood on my shoulders and Hope on his. Kira reached for another handhold but missed it.

"Kira, that ledge is too far. You're not going to make it.

Or you're going to die trying," I held my hands helplessly in the air, knowing that if she did fall, I'd never be able to catch her—maybe just break her fall.

The section of the wall on either side of her was sheer. She had run out of handholds. I moved up the loose gravel on the slope next to the base of the wall as quickly as I could.

"Not you too, Nate. Don't even think about it." Gran's voice cracked. She was desperate.

"I'm not climbing. I'm just getting under her." I held my hands high in the air. When I got directly beneath her, I could see Kira looking straight down between her legs at me. She had a determined look in her eyes.

Kira made another leap at a rock that was just out of her grasp. She missed and teetered on one foot.

"Ahhh…"

"Kira, don't move." I tried to climb the rocks to reach her but my foot slipped and my hands scraped down the rock face.

"Nate. Don't." I glanced back at Gran. Oz was surrounded by the rope that was always tied to his backpack.

"Nate, my fingers are so tired. I don't know how long I can hold on. I'm sorry. This was stupid."

"It's okay, Kira, we'll get you down." Although, I didn't know how.

"What are you doing, Oz?" I asked when I turned around.

He ignored me and called to Gran. She moved to his side, while Hope and I continued to stand shoulder to shoulder with our arms stretched above our heads.

Oz and Gran conferred before she took over and lashed

the rope around a boulder.

"Kira, just hang on. I saw this on Wildman," Oz said.

"Seriously, Oz. Enough with the Wildman nonsense. We don't have time for this." I was angry that he would joke when Kira was seriously in danger.

"This isn't nonsense. I'm not kidding around. Do you hear any Outback accents coming from me? Gran's securing one end of the rope on the boulder because that will be our anchor." Oz then tied knots about a foot apart on the other end before he lashed the free end around a rock about the size of my fist. In all the years we've known each other, I'd never seen Oz so focused.

Kira groaned above me.

"Just hang in there. Oz is almost done," I said.

Oz ran over to where Hope and I stood. "You're not going to like this part, Kira, but you have to trust me. I'm going to toss this rope up and over that ledge above your head. If it works, this rock will pull the rope down on the other side, and we can use the ledge to support your weight."

"Wait, wait." Kira breathed in and out quickly and shifted her weight on the teetering outcroppings. "Did you just say that you are tossing a rock at my head?"

"Well, yeah. But it's a small one. And it should go over you. Just duck if it comes close to your face."

Oz stepped back and flung the rope up into the air. He looked like Batman tossing a grappling hook onto a building. The rock missed the ledge and crashed down next to Kira. She screamed as one of her feet slipped off the rock when she ducked.

"KIRA, DON'T MOVE." I said it quietly to keep her calm.

"Then don't throw the rock so close to me!"

"Sorry. It usually takes Wildman a few tries too," Oz said.

"But he's not throwing it at someone's head, is he?" I asked.

"Good point. I promise I'll get it this time, Kira." Oz backed away from the wall and stared.

"Nate, can you get me any higher?" He climbed up my back and wrapped his legs over my shoulders. Oz drew his arm behind his head, flung it forward, and let go of the rock. The rope unwound as it flew. It cleared the ledge and six feet of rope dropped off the other side.

"Yes!" Oz hopped down and ran over to where the rope hung. "Gran, are you good back there?"

"I'm good, but hurry, Oz."

Gran knelt near the boulder where the rope was lashed, and Oz held onto to the end that pooled onto the ground. He jumped, and the rope pulled taut over the ledge and all the way down to the boulder. It held his weight.

"Okay, Kira. I know you're tired, but you need to grab this rope. Gran's end will support you. I tied big knots in the rope every few feet. Stand on them when you need to rest."

Kira grabbed the rope with both hands. She followed Oz's instructions, sighed heavily and rested her feet on a knot.

"I'm okay."

"You're not done yet, Kira, but we're here under you," I said. "Climb down the rope—just like in gym class. You've got this."

Oz squeezed between me and Hope and held his arms up in the air. Sweat dripped down his face.

"I'm coming." Kira eased her way down one knot at a time. After she reached our hands and collapsed into our arms, she threw herself at Oz and hugged him around the waist.

"I will never doubt you again, Oz—or Wildman. I don't even know how you thought of that," Kira said.

Oz's face turned bright red. "Well, I had some help from Gran, too."

"I didn't do much, Oz. You're the true hero. We should all be glad that you were here." Gran put her arm around Oz. I nudged his other side with my elbow.

"I'm sorry I doubted you. That was awesome," I said.

"It's all good, mate," Oz said in his ridiculous Australian accent. He grinned and wound his rope into a pile.

We sat on the ground for several minutes so that everyone's hearts could stop racing. My hands finally stopped shaking.

"Please don't ever do anything foolish like that again, Kira." Gran hugged her.

"I won't, I promise. But I'm still sure there were babies up there."

We were all drained of energy, so it was good that the Tonto Trail wasn't steep. It was rocky, though. We had to watch where we put our feet because these short barrel-shaped cacti stuck up from between the rocks on the trail. It was much different from the dusty dirt paths we had been on before. We kept our eyes open for cairns, manmade piles of rocks that were stacked along the trail, to mark the way. I asked Hope to walk with me in the front of the group because she was good at spotting the cairns. I made sure we stayed on the right route.

We made a sharp left around a rock tower and into a narrow canyon. While Hope scouted in front, Kira eyed the wall to our left and looked for another condor cave that might be within climbing distance. Gran and Oz were each using a trekking pole to navigate the rocks. I could hear Gran tell Oz about tying a clove hitch knot around the boulder. With my eyes turned away to the side, I almost ran right into Hope when she stopped in the middle of the trail.

Three bighorn sheep stood in front of us. I shouldn't have been surprised because there were piles of poop all along the Tonto. Gran thought it was mountain lion scat. I had read that a baby bighorn sheep makes a tasty dinner for a mountain lion, and since May is the lambing season, there might be some helpless babies somewhere nearby.

"Maybe we've found our ungulates," I said.

Each sheep had small straight horns, so I figured they must be female because the males have giant curved ones. Their coats were a grayish-brown and patchy in places like they were losing some hair. The sheep nudged aside rocks to dig into cactus and the low scrub brush along the trail. They didn't seem bothered by us.

Hope pointed to a wall in front of us. At the base, another female stood with two baby sheep next to her.

They moved around her legs and stopped to drink milk until they lost their footing on the loose stones. The toppled babies bleated loudly, and the mom hopped down the rocks to nudge them off the ground and back to safety.

"Look at how fast she moves. How is that even possible?" I asked.

"Didn't you see Oz jump into action? Animals move quickly when their family is in danger." Gran balanced her pack on a rock and pulled out her water bottle.

"You guys are definitely like family. But did I look that nervous too?" Oz asked.

The sheep jerked her head back and forth and scanned the horizon.

"You can't blame her. We're the biggest animals around, and she's used to big animals like eagles and mountain lions that want to mess with her babies. Let's keep walking so she can relax," Gran said.

Gran eased her backpack to the ground and knelt to put her arms through the straps. She stood up and hunched it onto her back, redistributing the weight.

"All this water I'm carrying threw me off balance."

If I'm being honest, everything about the day felt off balance. Kira getting stuck, Oz's rescue, and still no confirmation on where we were headed. We'd hiked all morning and aside from two more black dots in the cliffs at least three hundred feet above us, I hadn't seen any signs of condors or anything else from the clue. I think everyone else felt the same way because even Hope, who never seemed to be bothered by the long distances, complained that her feet hurt.

After another half mile, we found ourselves at the entrance to Horn Creek Canyon. This was the first waterway along the Tonto. We hoped it would be our last. Horn Creek wasn't as dry as our guidebooks said it might be. It trickled down toward the Colorado River after the heavy rains a few days before. The book also said not to drink water from Horn Creek because it was radioactive due to natural uranium collected in a collapsed cave system upstream.

The water was clear and there were tiny fish swimming in it. I guess I expected that something radioactive would be oozing fluorescent yellow goop like that scene in Batman when the Joker falls into the vat of acid and his face gets sizzled. But, it looked like every other creek we had seen on this trip.

"Kira, you know about all this stuff. What happens to us if we drink this radioactive water?" I asked.

"You shouldn't ever drink it, but the truth is you would need to live here and drink only this water for a really long time for it to hurt you. In fact, back when Grand Canyon became a national park, the story goes that people sold radiated water and claimed it was a magical cure-all. But enough of it can give you cancer, so I think we should steer clear of it," Kira said so matter-of-factly as if she'd been studying radiation her whole life. I don't know how she has room for all those facts in her head.

"No problem. I've got plenty of my own water. I just didn't want to be glowing when we get out of here," I said.

"Speaking of glowing, check out that wall over there," said Oz.

The sun shot rays through the clouds, and a rock formation far in the distance glowed red. I traced our coordinates on my map and used my watch to confirm how long we had been on the trail.

"If I'm reading the map right," I pointed to the rock formation Oz had noticed, "that could be Cheops Pyramid."

"Wait, you mean we're here? This is it?" Oz dropped his pack on the ground and sighed expectantly. "Let's get started and find something."

I gave Kira Gramps' letter. She held it out in front of her, closed one eye, and used her hand to make an L-shape to frame the rock pyramid far in the distance. The formation matched the sketch with the number two perfectly, which was also the same as Mr. Strunk's photo we saw the night before.

"'In the end, you'll understand only one points the way.' So which way is it pointing?" she asked.

Kira lined herself up with the center of the formation and spun around to face the red cliffs behind us. "Redwall limestone. That's what this is. Nate, read back the whole clue."

I read the clue out loud with all of the answers filled in: "TONTO TRAIL will lead WEST to the point where the CHEOPS PYRAMID can be seen. REDWALL LIME-STONE is behind so make sure your eyes are keen. Within a crevice find a SPLIT-TWIG FIGURE, I left for you to

see, and right above I hope you see a NEST and then a ??
SOUND."

"You're right. This has to be it. We need to find a split-twig figure or maybe there's a nest that's easier to reach," I said.

Oz and I scrambled up the mound of scree at the base of the red wall. My eyes scanned every crevice back and forth like reading lines in a book. Left to right, left to right—to make sure I didn't miss anything. Oz used the same technique, but his head bobbed up and down like he was reading a column of numbers. Kira and Hope felt every ledge they could reach and brushed their hands over the rocks in an attempt to find a figure. Gran stayed lower on the ground and watched our every move.

"Just don't get any fancy climbing ideas, Kira," Gran said.

After fifteen minutes, we had barely covered one-third of the towering wall. I walked back to my pack to get a drink of water.

"Nothing. Gran, there is nothing here. This has to be the place. Don't you think we're right?"

"I do. I think you've done everything right, but maybe whatever Gramps left…whatever he saw…maybe it isn't here anymore."

"I don't believe that. We couldn't have made it all this way to find nothing."

"Nate," Gran's voice was quiet, "read the letter again. Gramps even said that you must have patience and he *hoped* you would find the mystery he discovered. And you, dear boy, aren't good at patience or hope."

"What about hope?" Hope heard her name and came up behind me.

"I was telling Nate that Gramps said we need to have patience and hope once we arrived. None of you are very patient, except maybe you, Hope."

"We haven't lost hope. I'm right here." Hope laughed.

I groaned at her joke and she guided me over to a rock where we sat. Oz and Kira climbed like spider monkeys over every inch of the wall they could reach.

After almost an hour, they stopped searching, too. When they walked back to where Hope and I sat, I could see that their hands and arms were scratched from the sand-papery surface of the rocks. They both plopped down and chugged from their water bottles. Hope sat motionless with her eyes on the sky.

"I don't see anything and there is nothing in any of those crevices," she said.

"Okay, let's rethink this. Maybe this isn't the right wall. Maybe we haven't gone far enough," I said.

Tears streamed down Kira's dirt-covered cheeks. We were all frustrated. We knew we were close and obviously just missing something. After six days, we couldn't face another obstacle. Gran was the only one who seemed calm. Maybe after all those years being married to Gramps some of his stubborn patience had worn off on her. She seemed perfectly happy to sit under the shade of the tree at the campsite beside Horn Creek and stare up into the sky.

"Look." Gran stood up and pointed at a bird circling above us.

IT WAS THE SAME KIND of black bird that had circled over me at the river. Same long wings and short neck.

"Another turkey vulture. Man, those things are everywhere." Oz shaded his eyes to see the bird above us.

"No." Kira felt blindly in her pack for her binoculars, never letting her eyes leave the sky. "Look at the white under the wings. That's a condor. I knew it. I knew Gramps wouldn't lead us astray."

She looked so happy. Then I remembered that after searching the whole trip, this was the first condor that Kira had seen up close in the wild. The bird dove behind the tower in front of us.

"Well, don't just sit there. Let's go see," I said. It took us ten minutes to get to the other side of the rock wall. We were all trying to run, and Gran was chasing after us, her arms filled with water bottles. When we finally spotted the condor again, it was thrusting its head into something on the ground. A carcass.

"What is that?" Oz asked.

162

"Looks like it was pretty big," Hope said softly. "I'm guessing that condor is enjoying a mountain lion's sloppy seconds."

We made sure to stay away from the bird by at least the distance of a football field. It filled its beak with meat pulled from the dead animal and lifted off the ground with one beat of its wings. High above us on the Redwall Limestone wall, I noticed another black hole—a cave.

The bird rose noiselessly up, and I could just barely see it perched in the opening of the cave.

"It's probably feeding a baby up there. I think that's the nest," Kira said desperately.

"Don't even think about climbing, Kira. I'm not rescuing you twice today," Oz said.

Kira looked exasperated. "Will you at least take a picture then?"

Oz pulled his phone from his pocket and fumbled with the screen.

"Hang on." Oz shaded the phone from the sun reflecting off it. "I can't see anything." He punched at the screen.

A noise blared from the phone—it was the chainsaw noise of his snoring and then the strange dog barking in the background.

"Ah, dude." Oz fumbled with his phone, pounding on the screen. "Sorry, hang on. I can't even see the buttons." He pushed the screen and the sound came out again, like a puppy yipping.

"*Wooh, wooh, wooh, wooh…wooh*," followed by silence and then crickets in the background.

"Nevermind, Oz. The condor's gone. It must be inside

the cave." Kira was out of breath and sank to the ground with her face in her hands. Hope and I stood next to Gran. Our silence was broken by another sound, "*Oooo-woo.*"

"Enough, Oz. Shut it off okay," Kira whispered. Oz turned his phone over and poked the screen a few more times.

"That wasn't me. I swear. I shut it off."

We heard the second noise again, this time above us.

Kira looked up from her hands and turned to face the wall. "Oz, play it again."

"I thought you were sick of it."

"Just play it, please." He played back the recording and we all watched Kira who was watching the wall. When it got to the part of the recording with the yipping sound, Oz slid his finger over the screen and played it twice more. We waited.

"*Ooo-woo,*" echoed from above us.

"That sound is coming from up there," Kira said.

We all scanned the wall and looked for the source of the noise. Could a mountain lion cub be hiding in the rocks? My eyes stopped on something just above our heads. Balanced on a ledge was a cairn, no taller than my forearm. Poking out from under it was a pile of sticks.

"It's a cairn," I said.

"Someone put a cairn up there?" Oz asked in an astonished tone.

I climbed a few feet and stretched my hand and pulled out the pile of sticks.

"Not someone," I said. "Gramps." I jumped the final few feet to the ground. Inside my clutched fist were three split-twig figures, carefully twisted. They were dry and rigid, not flexible like the one I made the day before.

I laughed out loud. It was like holding a secret message from Gramps in my hand. "It was definitely Gramps, and I guess I get my lack of split-twig skills from him. He wasn't very good at making those bighorn sheep either."

Hope took one of the willow animals and turned it over. "That's not a sheep, Nate. It looks like an owl to me."

She held it upright so that I could see two carefully outlined round eyes and a circular head with an oval-shaped body beneath. Once Hope said it, I could clearly see that it was an owl. I peered up to the crevice where the cairn was sitting, but I didn't see any signs of life.

"Oz, let's hear it one more time." Oz dragged his finger across the screen and let it play again. We all held our breath and watched the motionless wall in front of it.

What seemed like ten minutes passed, but then I noticed movement directly above the ledge where the cairn had been. A round face peered over the edge. It was brown with white polka dots, smooth around the edges, and fuzzy in the middle near the dark eyes. A bright yellow beak was in the center of its face. It was an owl—just like the figures.

The owl looked like it had been taking a nap. It blinked. I walked backward and never took my eyes off the curious bird. When I was far enough back, I could see two more owls—one that looked just like the first, and another that was similar in size, but covered all over with a thick layer of fluff. The fluffy one bobbed its head up and down and its brown eyes stood out from the white feathers on its face.

I inhaled, afraid to make a sound and scare the birds.

"It's an owl," I whispered.

"A family of owls," Kira nudged me. The baby owl hobbled to the edge of the cavern where it was nesting. It moved its head up and down and extended its wings. In a split second, the owl raised itself up into the air. Its fat body looked too big to be supported by its slender wings. Like a fuzzy potato balancing underneath a paper airplane. It flapped its wings like it was trying them out for the first time, wobbled in the air, and landed hard in a crevice down below. It tucked one wing against its body and tried several times to get the other tucked back into place.

The owl spread its wings again, leaped from the rock, and flew back up to the others. The flapping of its wings looked stronger and more even this time. It landed near the older owls, who nudged it back into the safety of the crevice.

Hope was the first one to break our silence.

"I think it's learning to fly," she said. "Trying out its wings."

I held the split-twigs in my hand. I wasn't sure why Gramps had sent us to find these owls, but I knew this was exactly what we'd been searching for. We waited for them to reappear, but the rock face was motionless. With almost three miles back to Indian Gardens, and our water running low, we knew that it was time to head back to camp.

"We should go," I said.

The trek took an hour. Kira walked by herself at the back of the group. I let Oz and Hope pass us by.

"What's wrong?" I asked.

"I just don't understand. Why would he send us all this way and have us look for an owl?" she asked.

"Gramps was an ornithologist, not just a condor specialist, Kira. There must be something special about those owls." I began to feel a sense of pride. We had survived six days of brutal hiking, dodged rattlesnakes and flash floods, and we finally found what Gramps sent us to look for.

"And besides. You got to see your condor. If we hadn't followed it around the rock face, we would never have found the owls. It's almost like that condor was leading us to them."

Kira's face changed. She stopped to look behind us and put her hands on her hips. "You know, you're right. We would never have found any of it without the condors."

When we finally arrived at camp, we saw Mr. Strunk.

He sat at his site's picnic table scrolling through photos.

"Nate and crew, how was your hike today? Did you find what you were looking for?"

"Yes," we all said at once. I'm certain we answered 'yes' for different reasons, though.

"What did you find?" Mr. Strunk asked.

"It was an owl. A family of owls, actually. They were brown with white spots and these big brown eyes, and they were nesting up in a shady hollow in the side of a rock," I said.

Mr. Strunk held a finger up in the air and darted inside his tent. He returned with his bag, flipped open the bottom of his camera, and switched out the memory card. His fingers pushed quickly. He looked excited.

"I know just the type you mean. Is it this little guy?" He held up his camera so that I could see a photo of an owl almost identical to our find. This one was perched on a tree branch with thick forest behind it.

"That's it."

"Those are the Mexican spotted owls," Mr. Strunk said. "They're a threatened species, so there aren't that many left in the world."

Oz and Hope crowded around the camera. "But that one is in a tree. Where did you take this picture?"

"At my campsite on the North Rim last week. And boy, those owls must have been having some sort of territorial dispute. This one was making a racket all night. Sounded like my puppy barking at the back door."

We all looked at each other and smiled. Oz held up his phone and we all knew it was the same noise we heard on our first night in camp.

"But why would Gramps lead us to these owls?" Kira asked.

"Now that's something that I can't tell you. Sounds like a mysterious guy, that grandfather of yours. Maybe you should ask your grandmother." Mr. Strunk set down his camera and pointed at Gran's shirt. "I noticed that she wears an owl charm on her necklace."

Gran gasped and her eyes filled with tears. She grabbed the charm and pulled it back and forth on its chain.

"I forgot all about this. I always thought he gave it to me as a symbol of love because owls mate for life. I should have known that Gramps always intended for us to find owls out here, and this was the only way he could tell me without giving it away. It was his last message to all of us."

Kira shook her head. "But I still don't understand why."

"I bet I know someone," Gran said, "who can tell us the rest of the story…"

CHAPTER

19

OZ AND I STAYED AWAKE most of the
night wondering who Gran was talking about. Just as the
sun rose, I realized it must be Kelly Bartlett, the wildlife
biologist. We already had plans to meet her at the South
Rim. I was anxious to finish the 4.8-mile trip from Indian
Garden to the top.

I seemed to be the only one, though.

Oz groaned when our alarm buzzed.

"I can't hike anymore." He handed me his phone. "Use
this to signal for a rescue helicopter."

I shook him and held the buzzing phone up to his ear.

"Time to get up. I thought you were dying for that ice
cream. It's waiting for you on the South Rim."

Oz shot up. He was dressed and out of the tent before I
could stuff my sleeping bag into its sack.

"Hope. Kira. Wake up. A double-chocolate swirl delight
is calling my name from up there." Oz pointed both hands
at the sheer red cliff at the end of the valley.

Kira's head poked out of the girls' tent. Her glasses sat
crooked on her nose, and Hope was behind her with hair

sticking out in every direction.

"Right now?" Kira asked.

"Right now. The captain says that the ship sails in fifteen minutes." Oz tossed me a salute and waved at Gran who was boiling water for breakfast.

The skies were overcast, and I was thankful for a cool morning. Ahead of us, the flat trail disappeared quickly. We were faced with an endless series of switchbacks on a section called Jacob's Ladder.

"This is going to be the hardest day of our trip. I can feel it," Kira said.

"Why don't I read you what we have finished in our legend? That might help pass the time," I said.

"Anything to distract us from another switchback." Oz leaned against the canyon wall to catch his breath.

I turned to a page in my notebook and read:

"When the elder was near the end of his life, he spoke to his people. He said it was time for them to journey into the great canyon—"

"Gimme that." Oz snatched my notebook and read silently. "That's what you guys have been working on the whole time? If the rest of it is as boring as this—"

"Oz, don't be mean. Nate worked hard on that." Kira counted out ten more steps, sat down, and sprawled her long legs in front of her.

"Nate is the best writer in our class. He writes these epic adventure stories."

"That's what this is, Oz." I wiped sweat out of my eyes.

"No, it's not. You missed all the action that makes your stories so great. Don't try so hard." Oz tossed me the notebook and started up the trail.

I wondered if he was right. Words usually flowed onto the page for me, but writing this legend had been like waiting for honey to drip out of the bottle. I jogged forward to catch up with him.

"Maybe you're right. Let's start again. Everybody, tell me your favorite part of the trip." I turned to the last page in my notebook and recorded their responses.

"Seeing my first condor." Kira looked through her binoculars and swerved to the edge of the trail. Oz grabbed the strap on Kira's backpack and pulled her to the middle.

"Rescuing Kira and drinking water from my sock. I didn't know if all those things I learned from Wildman would actually work," he said.

"Surviving the canyon with my family." Gran pointed to Oz and Hope. "You, too. Not just my blood relatives."

"Helping that lizard get out of Gran's tent in one piece." Hope laughed.

"What about you, Captain?" Oz asked.

I stopped at a sign for the Three Mile Resthouse. "Solving the treasure hunt, of course."

The Three Mile Resthouse was a covered shelter with stone benches. Gran and the girls talked to a ranger who was patrolling the area. Oz filled up our water bottles and I wrote in my notebook.

When we left, we passed a group of people working on the trail. They were dressed in heavy boots, canvas gloves, and green hard hats. Two volunteers with shin guards like we wear for soccer, moved rocks to the edge of the trail to create a stone guardrail. The others shoveled red dirt into potholed sections of the trail.

All the way up the steep winding section, we took breaks every five minutes. I counted my steps silently: one through twenty…sometimes trying to get to twenty-five before I stopped again.

"I took your advice, Oz. I'm writing an epic adventure story instead. Want to hear it?"

Four breathless 'Ayes' sounded from behind me. I cleared my throat and read:

"A short time ago in a canyon far, far away…A band of voyagers declared their intentions to explore—"

"That sounds like Star Wars. That's even better than a super hero story. Nate, you're a genius," Oz said.

I stretched my calves, balanced the notebook in one hand, and pushed against the canyon wall with my legs behind me.

"Can I continue?"

"By all means, Captain." Oz saluted.

"A band of voyagers declared their intentions to explore the reaches of the vast canyon by following the Path of the Thunderbird. The adventurers must return home in seven days or face great peril as their food dwindles and their desire for sweet snacks overwhelms them."

"Are you talking about Oz's sweet tooth?" Gran asked. I nodded. "Perfect," she said.

"The Path of the Thunderbird. How did you come up with that?" Of course, Kira would pick up on the condor part.

"Last night, I marked all of the trails we traveled." I fished the map from the outer pocket of my pack.

"This green line is our path: starting at the South Rim, around to the North Rim, and down the main corridor of the canyon, with a few side trips." I traced the line around the map.

"I get it. We saw the ranger tracking condors here." Kira pointed to the Battleship Mesa. "The condors are released from Vermilion Cliffs and fly back down to the caves on the Tonto Trail. Why didn't I think of this? We've been following the path of the condor all along."

"Sometimes it takes a great navigator to notice something like that." They groaned, but Gran nodded.

Kira and Hope pushed forward with steady steps. "Read us more…"

We made it to the Mile-and-a-Half Resthouse, and through the first stone tunnel by 9:15 a.m. I looked back down at Plateau Point in the distance and realized that everything was starting to look familiar.

"We've been here before. We must be getting close. Oz, see if your phone has a signal," I said.

"I don't remember this at all. Are you sure we've been here?" Oz fiddled with his phone.

"Well, *we* have, Oz, but you were too busy scaring us half to death." Gran put her arm around Oz.

"Oh yeah." Oz wouldn't look at us. "No signal yet."

Between the first and second tunnels, a group of kids in matching t-shirts took pictures of a rock wall on our right. Near the top were drawings in orangey-red paint the color of the trail dust.

"Those are American Indian pictographs or rock writings, probably drawn by the ancient people who walked this trail down to Indian Garden," Gran said.

There was a lizard, a snake, an ungulate: maybe a bighorn sheep, some footprints, and a spiral symbol.

"We saw all those animals in the canyon, and that spiral is like us, walking in circles for days," Kira said.

A man stopped next to us and read from his guidebook. "Many people believe that the spiral symbolizes water."

I put my own water bottle up to my mouth and thought about the Colorado River wearing away the rock over millions of years to form Grand Canyon. It made sense to me that the American Indians would include that in their art.

We passed through the final rock tunnel, and I knew we would reach the rim after the next turn. People walked down the trail in clumps, slipped on their flip flops, and huffed and puffed. Even though I could barely lift my feet, I felt so different than I had the week before. Like the canyon was now a part of me. We all ran the final steps to the top, except Gran, who still put her trekking poles in front of her at an even pace.

Oz messaged Kelly, who responded that she would take the shuttle and meet us at the trailhead. The first thing I noticed when Kelly arrived was the envelope in her hand. She smiled and hugged each of us.

"You made it! I'm so proud of you," she said.

We found some shade and spent the next hour telling Kelly about our adventure. Oz played his recordings, and I showed her my notebook. When I got to the part about the owls, Kelly interrupted me.

"They were there? How many?" Kelly bounced in her seat like Kira when she saw the condor.

"Three. One was really fluffy," I said.

"A baby, too? Your grandfather had a feeling the owls would be back," Kelly said.

"But we don't understand. I thought Gramps was studying the condors." Kira looked frustrated as though her animals were being left out.

"He was, Kira. But your grandfather was an ornithologist. He didn't only study the condors, he was researching all the raptors in the canyon, including the Mexican spotted owl."

"Here's the thing." Oz looked serious. "I understand that there are only four hundred condors in the world, and people have spent a ton of time trying to get them to breed in the wild. But what's the story with these owls? Why did Gramps think they were even more important?"

"Definitely not more important, Oz. Just different. The condors lived in the canyon 10,000 years ago. This is a natural home for them. However, the Mexican spotted owl traditionally lives in old-growth forests, like where you camped on the North Rim."

Kelly continued, "There are wildfires happening all over the western United States, and when the forests burn, the owls are uprooted. Over time, a small percentage of the Mexican spotted owls in the Southwest have adapted and now live in the steep canyons here. These owls are special because they have learned to survive in a place that wasn't their home."

"Kind of like us," Oz said. "Grand Canyon is nothing like Chicago, but we managed to survive."

Kelly laughed. "Exactly, but *you* were responsible for your own safety down there. Grand Canyon was declared a Globally Important Bird Area by the National Audubon Society, so *we* are responsible for the safety of the birds. As caretakers of the Mexican spotted owl, the condor, and another bird called the pinyon jay, we are trying to learn as much as we can about them."

"Is that something I could help with?" Kira peered through her glasses at Kelly. "I mean, a career in species preservation would be even better than ornithology."

"I agree. That's why I'm a wildlife biologist. I get to learn about how to protect many types of animals in the park," Kelly said. "Your grandfather and I monitored this pair of owls. For two years, they returned to the same nesting spot, but then we didn't see them again. This isn't uncommon because owls don't lay eggs every year. He thought if they returned this year, it would be a sign that the canyon had become a safe place for them to nest. The canyon is a sanctuary to so many animals. Our job is to figure out ways to protect them."

Kelly turned to the final page of my notebook and raised her eyebrows while she read. Our story wasn't finished yet, but after talking to her, the ending was becoming more clear.

She looked up. "There's one more thing. Your grandfather asked me to give you this envelope when you finished your hike. Nate, will you do the honors?"

I TORE THE ENVELOPE OPEN AND
unfolded a letter that was covered in Gramps' scratchy writing. I read it, grabbed my notebook, and wrote for several minutes.

"Nate, what are you doing? We want to read Gramps' letter." Kira tried to grab it from my hand.

"Wait a minute. Gramps' letter provided the perfect ending to our legend. Let me read this to you first." I cleared my throat and read:

The Path of the Thunderbird

A short time ago in a canyon far, far away…

A band of voyagers declared their intentions to explore the reaches of the vast canyon by following the Path of the Thunderbird. The adventurers must return home in seven days or face great peril as their food dwindles and their desire for sweet snacks overwhelms them. Although they are armed with the best equipment, these mighty explorers have no idea of the scorching heat and dangerous terrain they must conquer.

The Wise One, who traveled to another universe, provided the canyon buccaneers with a puzzle, the key to their mission: a quest to uncover the treasures of this desert chasm. The Captain leads the explorers on a brave hunt and chronicles the group's discoveries in his sacred book.

The canyon's sinister agents: a crazed mule, ravenous squirrels, and thieving ringtail cats attempt to block the travelers from their mission.

The coiled pink rattler, obsessed with finding its prey, and the shifty bobcat, intent on terrifying them with its deafening scream, pursue the explorers into the depths of the canyon.

A painted lizard breaches the fortress of the graying Elder, desperate to find shelter for her offspring. In a stunning move, the Naturalist from the southern reaches of the galaxy, coaxes the creature away from the temptations of the human world.

The voyagers remain vigilant in their quest until the mighty Thunderbird unleashes its power, filling the skies with lightning and disrupting peace and order in the canyon.

On a remote path, a lost wanderer crumbles under the canyon forces. In a heroic rescue, the adventurers use their new-found knowledge to save the battered wayfarer.

In a desperate attempt to locate the Thunderbird, the Scientist is trapped on a treacherous ledge. She narrowly escapes sudden death when the Australian Survivalist aims projectiles at her, rescuing her from a harrowing fate on the cliffs.

The travelers meet a trusted ally, the Image Maker, who retrieves the Captain's book of wisdom lost among the rocks. Without it, they would never decipher the final clue leading to the whereabouts of the treasure.

Little do the adventurers know, the treasure is an owl whose survival is threatened by forces of the galaxy beyond its control. Driven to the wild depths of the canyon, this bird created a home more protected and beautiful than its native land. Like the owl, the voyagers have been forced to adapt to their own foreign surroundings.

The Scientist realizes her mission extends beyond the preservation of the Thunderbird to include all creatures who may benefit from her knowledge. The Captain seeks counsel from others to ensure the safety of his crew and the success of their quest. The Naturalist shares wisdom and her tribe's traditions to strengthen the bonds of this family of explorers. The Survivalist proves that his understanding of the skills passed down from his Master is powerful when used in the wilds.

The Elder receives the greatest gift of all—another quest devised by the Wise One to ensure that the voyagers will fight for the survival of others threatened in the galaxy and throughout the universe …

"Did you say another quest? Give me the letter," Kira snatched Gramps' letter from my hand.

"Another trip? All of us?" Hope asked.

"Yes. Gramps' letter has instructions for the beginning of our next adventure in November," I said.

"You mean I have to spend my Thanksgiving with you crazy kids?" Gran smiled. I knew there was nothing that would make her happier.

"Seriously, I don't know if I can handle Oz's snoring again." Kira laughed.

"You all have six months to miss my awesome snoring," Oz said. "But for now, let's focus on the important things. Captain, you owe me some ice cream."

ACKNOWLEDGEMENTS

Thank you to Lillian (Lulu) Santamaria, Publisher; Theresa McMullan, Chief Operating Officer; and the entire staff of the Grand Canyon Association for recognizing the need for a middle grade novel that would ignite young people's imaginations and teach them about Grand Canyon.

Thanks to Amala Posey, Graciela Avila, and Andy Pearce, all environmental educators with the National Park Service; Janet Cohen, Tribal Program Manager; Gregory Holm, Wildlife Program Manager; and other members of Grand Canyon National Park's team for their input and expertise.

Thanks to the Peregrine Fund for its tireless efforts to reintroduce condors to the wild. We are grateful to the National Park Service staff and rangers who impart their enthusiasm for and knowledge about the precious resources and history that our national parks preserve and protect.

Thank you to David Jenney, art director/designer, for his support of the project from the beginning. Thank you to Scott Brundage, illustrator extraordinaire, for breathing life into the characters of Nate, Kira, Hope, and Oz, and capturing the beauty of Grand Canyon in his illustrations.

We are eternally grateful to Theresa Howell for believing in our writing team and giving us the courage and guidance to complete the story and the freedom to explore Grand Canyon with our words. Without her, this book would not have happened.

Finally, words cannot describe how much the encouragement of our family and friends meant to us. Thanks to Ranger Jeff Wolin of Florissant Fossil Beds National Monument for his advice; Ben Miller for always laughing at Oz's antics and giving us the hugs we needed to keep writing; Alex Miller for being our first (and best) reader and providing opinions about how twelve-year-olds should (and should not) talk; Kevin Miller for being a constant source of support and a steady voice of reason when we were too busy listening to the voices in our heads; and Gary Toole for listening to countless hours of research and for being the best cheerleader a book could have.

SARA MILLER is a fiction and nonfiction writer who has penned her own column for a suburban-Denver newspaper for more than a decade. Sara's fiction-writing interests include middle grade and young adult literature with a focus on outdoor adventures and unique voices that grab her readers. Sara currently works as a freelance writer and marketing professional for nonprofits. Sara lives in Colorado with her husband and two sons who love to ski and hike. She has visited more than 100 national parks, monuments, preserves, and memorials, and ranks her explorations of Grand Canyon and her first cold glass of lemonade at Phantom Ranch as some of her favorites.

PAT TOOLE is a former elementary/middle school social studies teacher with a Masters degree in Education in Curriculum and Instruction. Pat has traveled extensively to UNESCO World Heritage and National Park Service sites, like Grand Canyon, in search of settings for her stories. Whether examining Puebloan rock art drawings and ruins, walking among ancient man-made earthen mounds, or playing a game of Hawaiian checkers called Konane, Pat is eager to share her adventures and inspire young people to investigate the history and mysteries of our earth's cultural landscapes. Pat is a member of SCBWI and lives in Colorado with her husband.

Readers can find more information at
www.pathofthethunderbird.com

Grand Canyon Association